WEIGHTED BLISS

Inspired by a true story

Regina Chavez-Boon

311 North Enterprise

2025

Published by 311 North Enterprise.

This book is a work of narrative nonfiction based on the author's lived experiences. Individuals' names and identifying characteristics have been changed to protect their privacy. It reflects the author's present recollections of experiences over time. Some names and characteristics have been changed, some events have been dramatized to serve the narrative.

Cover concept developed by Regina Chavez-Boon in collaboration with ChatGPT.

Edited by Evelyn Boon

First Printing 2025

ISBN: 979-8-218-65937-0

Printed in the United States of America

Words can't always express the gratitude that lives deep
in the heart.
While my faith has kept me anchored, the love and support of my family and friends have carried me through more than they'll ever know. I am deeply blessed and endlessly grateful.

To my "Simon," I would never have believed in love at first sight if not for you. You were the start of something I never expected… and somehow, the place I still feel most at home.

Contents

ONE

NOT ONLY IN MY DREAMS

Angie stood in the middle of the highway, the wind whipping around her, tugging at her hair. The sun beat down on her skin, bright and relentless, casting a stark glare over the familiar stretch of road. It looked like Highway 33, one of those windy back roads threading through the hills of Ventura County. She squinted, scanning the road. Trees lined the edges of the asphalt, their leaves dancing in the breeze as loose dirt and gravel tumbled across the road.

But Angie wasn't paying attention to any of that. Her mind was buzzing, her heart pounding in sync with the high-pitched roar that filled the air. Two motorcycles. She recognized the sound of them even before they came into view, the unmistakable sound of Suzuki GSX-Rs. The first bike rounded the bend, streaking past her with a screech of tires. Angie instinctively clutched her ears, the noise too loud, too sharp.

Her stomach tightened as the second bike followed close behind, a blur of color and speed. Tony. Her brother. She knew it was him even before he removed his helmet, and the way he rode with such ease made it seem as if he was invincible.

But the road wasn't kind. Loose sand and gravel stretched across the asphalt, and in an instant, the first bike lost its grip. Angie's breath caught as she watched the rider skid, the machine slipping out from under him. Time seemed to slow as the rider hit the pavement, his body folding in on itself. Angie gasped as he was thrown from the bike, his body slammed down on the pavement before sliding over the embankment, tumbling down the slope, stopped by the thick brush a few feet down. The motorcycle continued past him, hurtling into a tree and meeting its dusty end in a spray of shattered bark and crumpled steel.

Her mind screamed, *Run*. But her feet felt rooted, weighed down by fear. She forced herself forward, her legs finally moving, but it wasn't fast enough. She hit the same sandy patch that had taken out the bike. She slipped, her body crashing towards the ground. But the earth beneath her wasn't sand anymore—it was pills. Prescription pills of all shapes and sizes were scattered across the ground like some strange, haunting confetti. They covered everything: the road, the brush, the embankment where the rider lay.

Angie's heart raced as panic set in. She couldn't see the rider. He was gone. The sky above darkened, storm clouds rolling in out of nowhere. The sunlight vanished, replaced by a suffocating darkness. She called out, but her voice didn't carry. The pills swallowed the sound just as they swallowed everything else.

The rider was gone.

Angie jolted awake, her breath shallow, her eyes wide and wild as they darted around the room. For a moment, she wasn't sure if she was still there on that highway, surrounded by the chaos of the dream. But no. She was in her bedroom. Safe. The morning light fell softly across the room, illuminating the familiar, a pair of twin beds, her desk, the dresser she'd inherited from her late grandmother. A cool ocean breeze drifted in, and the flutter of the curtain carried a faint saltiness of the sea, brushing against her face like a gentle wake-up call. But her heart still raced, the remnants of the dream clinging to her like a shadow.

She closed her eyes for a moment, forcing herself to take a few steady breaths. In through the nose, out through the mouth. The dream was still vivid in her mind, each detail sharp and unrelenting. She could still feel the pills beneath her, the terror of losing control.

But this was reality. And she needed to shake it off.

It was September 2004–six months until the wedding. Angie turned her head toward the other bed in the room, neatly made and covered with a spread of wedding planning chaos: magazines, to-do lists, a pile of invitations waiting to be mailed. Her eyes flicked to her engagement ring, the diamond catching the sunlight and sparkling like a promise.

Simon. She needed to hear his voice, needed the grounding comfort that only he could provide. Her fingers found her phone on the nightstand, her Nokia 3310 bringing her back to the present. She dialed without hesitation.

Two

Not So Picture Perfect

The ringtone of Simon's matching Nokia jolted Angie out of her thoughts. She smiled as she heard his voice through the receiver, deep and comforting, like always.

"Well, good morning, future husband," she said with a playful cheer. The nickname felt like an anchor to the promise of what was coming, a life together, a new chapter. It warmed her in a way few things could.

"Good morning to you, future misses," Simon replied, his tone easy and familiar. The way they teased each other, even through the phone, made Angie's heart flutter. She pictured him in the car bay at Blazin' Audio, Ventura's premiere choice for stereo installation. He was probably working on some giant truck, expertly weaving wires and humming along to the music blasting in the background, just the kind of project he loved.

"I'm just calling to..." Angie started, knowing he'd jump in before she finished the thought.

"Remind me that I need to meet you at the beach by four P.M." Simon was always a step ahead, even in moments like this. He knew how much she wanted everything to be perfect.

"Exactly," she replied, her smile widening. "Lifeguard tower number?"

"Seventeen," Simon said without missing a beat, "where we first made out."

A brief, happy silence passed between them, filled with the unspoken memories of that first kiss. Angie held onto it for a second longer than usual, needing to feel its warmth.

"Uh huh," she whispered.

"I love you," Simon said. There was something in his voice, almost as if he was reminding himself.

"I love you too," Angie replied, and for a second, everything felt right.

She hung up the phone, but a small knot began to form in her stomach. *Don't overthink it,* she told herself. Simon would be there, like always. Sure, the car projects ran long sometimes, but today was special. They had the photographer lined up, her hair and makeup appointment double checked, and she'd be wearing her favorite fitted jeans. Today would be perfect. *It had to be.*

Simon leaned against the Chevy Silverado, wincing slightly as he shifted his weight. His back had been killing him lately, a constant reminder of the injury he had never fully recovered from. He glanced over at the open lid of his tool chest. The picture of Angie smiled back at him from the corner. It was a small photo, nothing fancy, but seeing her made the pain bearable. Next to it, a family portrait stared out at him, his parents, Susan and Hank, with their warm, reassuring smiles. His brother Jared, ever the clown, had Simon in a headlock in the photo, a moment of sibling chaos frozen in time. But that wasn't what bothered him.

What bothered him was the discomfort that seemed to settle in his bones lately, like he was always slightly off balance. He couldn't stand up straight, and the pain wasn't just in his back anymore; it was in everything. He sighed as he opened the top drawer of his chest and pulled out the familiar prescription bottle. The sound of the pills rattling inside was too familiar, too easy. He popped three Vicodins into his mouth and took them dry before returning to work.

The beach was breathtaking in the late afternoon, with the sun hanging low in the sky, casting everything in golden light. Angie stood by the water with Rene, the photographer, her eyes drifting toward the row of parked cars. She scanned the road, waiting, expecting to see Simon's truck pull up any minute now. The air was thick with that awkward silence, the kind that felt louder the longer it stretched.

"Looks like a lovely sunset setting in," Angie said, trying to break the tension. She smiled at Rene, but her heart was starting to race. Where was Simon?

Rene, ever the professional, checked her light meters. "Yeah. Never a bad sunset."

Angie forced another smile, but her mind was elsewhere. Simon should have been here by now. It wasn't like him to be late for something like this. She pulled her phone out and dialed again. *He's probably just a few minutes late. It's fine. He said he'd be here.*

As the phone rang, her stomach tightened. She tried to keep her tone light, but her nerves were betraying her. "I'll go ahead and call him, again."

Simon sat slumped behind the wheel of his truck, parked in front of his house. His head bobbed low like a balloon, losing its last lift. He could hear the phone ringing somewhere, but it took him a minute to realize it was his. Slowly, his eyes opened, blinking as if trying to fight off the sleep that kept tugging at him. He reached for the phone, his fingers fumbling before he finally answered.

"Heeeylow?" His voice was groggy, barely coherent.

"Simon," came Angie's voice, sounding distant and frantic. "Are you almost here?"

"Who this be?" Simon mumbled, not really registering the question.

Angie stepped away from Rene, lowering her voice for privacy. "It's Angie. Are you on your way?"

There was a long pause as Simon struggled to make sense of the conversation. "Why, where?"

"To the beach," Angie's voice cracked just slightly. "Are you feeling okay?"

She could feel the tears welling up in her eyes, and she quickly fanned her face, hoping to stop them before her makeup ran. *Stay calm*, she told herself. But Simon's slurred words weren't helping.

"Damn skippy hippy," Simon muttered, barely making sense.

"Si," Angie's voice broke, her patience fraying, "I need you to get here right now. Tower Seventeen. Please."

Simon mumbled something incoherent, but eventually managed, "Okay, I'm be right there."

Angie took a shaky breath, trying to steady herself as she turned back to Rene. The photographer's expression softened; she could tell something was wrong.

"Yeah, he got a little held up," Angie said, her voice strained. "He's on the way."

Rene glanced at her watch but said nothing, just giving Angie a reassuring nod. Angie appreciated the gesture, but the disappointment pressing down on her. The sun was beginning to set, and the light was fading faster than she'd hoped.

Minutes passed in silence. Angie stared at the horizon, willing Simon to appear. The sky was changing, that golden glow starting to fade into deeper hues of orange and pink. *It's getting too late*, she thought, her heart sinking.

"I'm sorry, Rene," Angie said quietly, "I don't know what to do."

Rene gave her a sympathetic smile. "You know, let me take some shots of you! Your hair and makeup look great. Might as well get some photos while we wait."

Angie tried to smile, but it felt forced, brittle. Rene raised her camera and began snapping photos, directing her to pose this way and that. Angie went through the motions, but her mind was elsewhere. *Where is he?*

The sun dipped lower, and Angie's heart sank with it. The beach, the sunset, it was all slipping away. Just as she was about to give up, she spotted Simon's truck rounding the corner. Relief and anxiety hit her all at once. *Finally*.

But when Simon stepped out of the truck, wearing a black polo, jean shorts, and socks with sandals, Angie's heart sank again. He wasn't himself. His eyes were droopy, and he moved with a lethargy that screamed something was wrong.

"Simon!" Angie's voice was sharp. "Where are your jeans?"

Simon looked down at his outfit, confused. "What? This looks nice."

Rene stepped in quickly, trying to diffuse the tension. "Okay, lovebirds. Let's get started. We don't have much time left."

The light was fading fast, the golden glow of the sunset slipping into twilight. Angie stood stiffly, trying to focus on the sound of the waves as Rene snapped away, but all she could think about was Simon. He was standing next to her, but in every way that mattered, he wasn't there.

Rene clicked the shutter a few more times, her expression neutral, but Angie could see it in her eyes. She could see Simon's heavy lids, his unfocused gaze. He kept nodding off, his head drooping forward, only to snap back up again like a puppet on a broken string.

Tears pricked the corners of Angie's eyes, but she blinked them away, refusing the emotion that was on the verge of breaking. *Not now*, she told herself. *Not here*. But it was impossible to ignore the growing frustration and the ache in her chest. This was supposed to be their moment. This was supposed to be perfect.

Rene finally lowered the camera, taking a step back. "Okay, I think we got some good ones," she said, her voice gentle but with a hint of uncertainty.

Angie forced a smile. "Yeah, thanks." She knew Rene was only being polite. The reality of Simon's behavior hanging between them.

Rene turned the camera toward Angie, offering a small, sympathetic smile. "Let me show you."

But Angie couldn't bring herself to look. The embarrassment sat like a stone in her gut. She knew the pictures wouldn't be what they had hoped for. Simon's dazed expression, the way he stumbled, half awake. She bit her lip, holding back the tears that threatened to spill over.

As Rene flipped through the shots, Simon wandered a few steps away, sinking down onto the sand with a grunt. He sat there, staring blankly at the horizon, his body slumped as if he could barely hold himself up.

Angie could feel the burn of embarrassment creeping up her neck. She turned back to Rene, her voice trembling slightly. "I'm so sorry, Rene. Um, he sometimes takes medication for his back pain. It doesn't always agree with him."

Rene paused, her eyes softening with understanding. "It's okay," she said kindly. "We can redo this session. I want you to have good pictures, ones you're happy with. We'll do this again, okay?"

Angie nodded, her throat tight with the effort of holding back tears. "Thank you," she whispered, grateful but feeling utterly embarrassed.

Rene reached out and touched her arm lightly. "Don't worry about it. I have some open dates coming up. Just give me a call, and we'll set it up."

Angie nodded again and gave a smile, she couldn't speak. She watched as Rene packed up her equipment, all the while feeling like everything had unraveled. She glanced over at Simon, still sitting on the sand, lost in his own haze. The pain in her chest twisted sharply, and she had to turn away before the tears could fall.

THREE

FAKE IT TILL YOU MAKE IT

Angie sat at the small desk in her bedroom, surrounded by bits of tulle and tiny white roses. She stared down at the mess of wedding favors scattered across the surface, little organza bags, half covered in hot glue, flowers that refused to stick where they should, and a wedding magazine splayed open to a picture of perfection she was failing to recreate.

She sighed in frustration, struggling with the glue gun. Her fingers burned as the hot glue oozed through the delicate fabric and pooled onto the desk. The more she tried, the worse it seemed to get. It wasn't like the picture. *Why can't I just get this right?* She huffed and dropped the glue gun, massaging her burned fingers, but the irritation gnawed at her.

Suddenly, her phone rang, breaking the tense silence. She glanced at the screen, Rosie. A flicker of relief passed through her. Talking to her sister always made things feel better, even if only for a moment.

Rosie was halfway across the world, stationed in some remote desert army base, cleaning out her footlocker in a barracks that probably had no windows. Even through the phone, Angie could hear the fatigue in her voice.

"Hey, sis!" Rosie's familiar cheerfulness shone through despite the exhaustion Angie knew she must be feeling.

"Hey, Rosie!" Angie replied, trying to sound more upbeat than she felt. "Shouldn't you be sleeping?"

Rosie chuckled softly. "Yeah, it's like tomorrow over here, but I couldn't sleep. I wanted to see how your pictures went?"

Angie froze for a second, her fingers tangled in the fine, sticky web of hot glue strings. The truth, sharp and painful, sat like a lump in her throat. How could she tell Rosie what had really happened? How everything had gone so wrong?

"They... uh, we didn't do them yet." The lie came out too quickly, her voice wavering as she tried to keep it steady. "I mean, we were going to, but the photographer had a conflict."

"That's too bad," Rosie said, sounding genuinely disappointed.

Angie forced a tight smile, even though her sister couldn't see it. "Yeah."

The silence between them stretched on for a moment, and Angie could feel her chest tightening. She wanted to tell Rosie everything, about how Simon had shown up late and out of it, about the disappointment that was quickly overshadowing her wedding plans. But she held back. Rosie didn't need that right now. She was dealing with enough.

"And everything else is good?" Rosie asked, her voice gentle. "The planning stuff?"

Angie felt her lip quiver, the breakdown she had been holding back all day threatening to spill out. She clenched her jaw, refusing to let it happen. "It's... it's okay, you know. Keeping me busy." She forced a laugh. "I wish you were here. Then I could go full-on bridezilla on you."

Rosie laughed, her voice filled with warmth. "That would be more fun than this hellhole! Ugh, just a few more months. At least you have Mom to help you."

"Yeah," Angie agreed. "She's been great."

But as she looked around at the messy piles of wedding favors, the unfinished projects, and the discarded magazines, Angie felt it all crashing down on her. She wanted to say more, to tell Rosie how overwhelmed she was, how much she missed her, how none of this felt like it was supposed to. But the words wouldn't come.

"Anyways," she said, trying to sound nonchalant, "you better get some sleep."

Rosie sighed dramatically. "Fine, I'll try."

"I love you," Angie said.

"Love you too."

For a moment, neither of them hung up, holding onto the brief connection that spanned thousands of miles. It felt like a lifeline, one Angie didn't want to let go of just yet.

Rosie's voice broke the silence. "Hang up."

Angie smiled, a real one this time. "No, you."

"I called you. You hang up."

"I'm older. You have to hang up."

"Dork. Bye." Rosie laughed, the sound bringing a moment of peace to Angie's heart.

Angie put the phone down just as a few stray tears escaped, finally slipping down her cheeks. She wiped them away quickly, trying to keep herself together. But it was hard. Everything felt like it was piling up, one disappointment after another. The engagement pictures, the wedding favors,

Simon... it was all slipping through her fingers, and she didn't know how to stop it.

She glanced back at the mess on her desk, the half-finished projects, the glue still cooling in uneven puddles. It wasn't like the perfect images she had in her mind or the ones plastered all over the wedding magazines. None of it felt like what she had hoped for.

With a deep breath, Angie gathered up the ruined wedding favors and tossed them into the wastebasket beside her desk. She could always start over tomorrow.

Four

Hold On Tight

It wasn't too long ago that Angie had been in her bedroom, wrestling with the simplest of problems, putting together a bed frame. She could still picture herself sitting cross-legged on the floor, surrounded by the disassembled pieces, her fingers tracing the edges of the instruction booklet as she tried, in vain, to make sense of the diagrams.

Ikea furniture was supposed to be easy, right? But as she flipped through the instruction booklet for the hundredth time, she couldn't understand the directions. The words, the diagrams just weren't connecting for her.

With a sigh, she tossed the instructions aside and leaned back against the wall, her pj pants and tank top rumpled from the day of struggling with this so-called "easy assembly." She took a sip from her drink, trying to calm the irritation inside her. Beneath her, the faint sound of music drifted from the garage; today, it was 311. Tony was down there, working on something like he always did. The base of the music was comforting, a familiar part of home.

Just as Angie was contemplating calling it quits for the day, the rumbling sound of an engine grabbed her attention. Her head snapped toward the window as the growl of a '67 cherry red Chevy Nova rolled into view. The car was pristine, polished to a high shine that gleamed in the afternoon sun. *Nice,* she thought, admiring the classic beauty.

Then, the driver's door opened.

A guy stepped out, and Angie's breath caught. "Oh damn," she muttered to herself, leaning in closer to the window. "Driver's not so bad either."

Simon was tall, ruggedly handsome, and had that effortless cool that made her pulse quicken. She watched him for a beat, taking in the way he moved, the way he laughed at something Tony said, the ease with which he fit into the scene. Her heart fluttered.

Suddenly aware of her messy hair and sleep deprived face, Angie scrambled to her feet. *Presentable,* she told herself. *I need to look presentable.* She darted over to the mirror, fingers quickly pulling her hair back into a more decent ponytail, checking for any signs of her earlier frustration. She didn't have time for much else, but she had to at least look like she hadn't been wrestling with a bed frame for hours.

Taking a deep breath, Angie made her way downstairs, her heart thudding in her chest. She reached the door to the garage and hesitated. Opened it just enough to see Tony and Simon working on something, talking casually. The muffled music mixed with the sound of tools clinking. *Get it together,* she reminded herself. She closed the door again, leaned against it, and took another breath.

When she finally pulled it open and stepped into the garage. She wasn't usually this nervous, but something about Simon made her fidgety in a way she hadn't expected.

"Hey, Tony," she said, her voice a little higher than usual, "do you know when Mom's coming home?"

Tony barely looked up from what he was doing. "Nope."

Angie wasn't really looking for an answer, though. She was trying to get a better look at Simon. Her eyes kept flicking toward him, and when they finally met his gaze, she felt her cheeks warm. *Act normal, you're staring – stop staring*, she told herself. *Just act normal.*

"Oh, um... do you have a hammer?" she asked, fumbling for an excuse to stay. Her mind raced, but all she could think about was the mess of a bed frame waiting upstairs.

Tony chuckled and waved toward the tool chest. "Toolbox, duh. For what?"

"I'm trying to put that stupid bed together, but the instructions are in German or Swedish or something. I'm just gonna bang it all in place."

Simon's voice cut in. "Do you need help?"

Angie blinked, momentarily stunned that he was even talking to her. "Oh, um..." *Words, Angie. Find words.*

"I don't mind," Simon added with a small, easy smile. "Ikea, right? Sounds like Ikea."

"Yeah," Angie said, feeling her cheeks grow warmer by the second. "Ikea. I could definitely use some help."

Simon wiped his hands on a rag and walked over to her, and Angie's heart skipped a beat. He was even more handsome up close, his wavy hair slightly tousled and his smile making her forget, for a moment, that she was standing in a grease scented garage wearing her pj pants.

As he approached, Angie tried to act casual, but her insides were buzzing. "My room's upstairs," she said, almost too quickly. "You sure you don't mind?"

"Nope," Simon replied, "I like projects."

"I'm Angie, by the way," she added, realizing she hadn't introduced herself.

"Simon," he said with a nod, extending his hand.

Angie's pulse raced as she took his hand, the warmth of his touch sending a jolt of excitement through her. She tried not to giggle as they shook hands. *Don't be weird*, she reminded herself. "Simon. Nice to meet you."

"Likewise," he said, his smile making her heart flutter all over again.

Words, Angie. More words. "That's a nice car you have, Nova, right?" she said, embarrassed, as she realized she was still in her pj pants.

"Yeah, it's my dad's. He lets me take it out sometimes," Simon replied.

They headed up the stairs together, Angie walking slightly ahead to guide him. As they reached her room, she cringed inwardly at the mess she had made, bits of the bed frame scattered all over the floor like a failed attempt at a DIY project.

"Here's the mess I've made," she said with an awkward laugh, handing him the directions.

Simon took them, scanning the instructions quickly. "This isn't so bad," he said, already moving to the pieces and setting them up like he had done this a hundred times before.

Angie stood off to the side, trying not to stare as he worked. But she couldn't help it. Watching him piece together her chaotic mess with such ease was oddly captivating. She was impressed, and also, he was gorgeous, which didn't hurt.

"So," she said, her voice a little more confident now, "how do you guys know each other?"

Simon glanced up briefly as he tightened a screw. "Mutual friends, I guess. And now we work together."

"Oh cool, so you work at Blazin' Audio too?" Angie asked, leaning against the wall, trying to seem casual even though her heart was still racing.

"Yeah."

She chewed her lip for a moment, then said, "Well, that sucks that Tony's leaving for boot camp soon. I won't have any excuse to visit."

Simon looked up at her then, their eyes meeting for a moment longer than necessary. "You could visit me."

Angie's breath caught, and she felt her face flush again. Was he flirting with her? She blinked, suddenly unsure of what to say. "Would you like something to drink, Simon?" she asked, her voice a little shaky.

"Water would be fine," Simon replied, his smile genuine.

"Okay. I'll be right back," Angie said, grateful for the excuse to escape for a moment. Her heart was racing, and she needed a second to collect herself. "And thank you so much, I appreciate the help."

"Sure," Simon said, glancing back at the bed frame. Then he added, "Angie, before I forget. When Tony goes to boot camp, I'd like to take his truck and wax it up for him. Like sometime before he comes back home."

"Oh," Angie said, surprised. "Like a welcome home thing?"

"Yeah."

"You'd do that for my brother? That's sweet," Angie said, feeling a warmth bloom in her chest. *He's really something,* she thought.

"He's a cool cat," Simon said with a shrug, "but I'll need to call you to arrange that."

Angie's heart fluttered again. "Um, yeah. Sure, you can call me anytime. I'm always here... I mean, I live here. You can call me."

Simon smiled, clearly amused by her rambling. "Alright, that's cool."

Angie nodded, feeling a little silly but still riding the high of their connection. "I'll be right back."

As she left the room, a big, silly grin spread across her face. She couldn't help it. She felt like a teenager again, giddy and full of excitement.

But that was then, she reminded herself, blinking against the warmth of nostalgia. The memory faded like the tail end of 311's *Amber*, lingering but distant, leaving her heart aching for the simplicity of those early days.

FIVE

WHAT'S ONE MORE MESS?

The kettle hissed and steam began to rise, curling in lazy spirals that filled the small kitchen. Angie glanced over at Simon, seated at the kitchen table, his expression focused as he stuffed yet another envelope with one of their wedding invitations. The padding of two pillows beneath him was a subtle reminder of his ongoing struggle with his back pain, a problem that seemed to linger in the background of everything these days.

She turned her attention back to the tea cups on the counter, their dainty floral patterns a soft contrast to the growing tension in the room. Her heart felt burdened by the things unsaid. The strain of recent events still clung to her like a shadow, but for now, they had to focus on the wedding. They had to pretend that everything was moving forward just as planned.

Simon's voice broke the silence, his tone casual but firm. "I'm tellin' you, babe, it just makes sense. We want to save up for a house, right? Living with my parents is the fastest way to do it."

Angie sighed, sitting down at the table to address more envelopes. She knew he was right, but the thought of living with his parents made her skin crawl. "Ugh, I know," she said, frustration creeping into her voice, "but it would be *weird* for me, that's all."

Simon didn't look up, still focused on his task. "My parents love you."

Angie shook her head, tapping the pen against the stack of envelopes. "It's not that," she said, struggling to find the right words. "It's like... how are we supposed to do 'married stuff' with them in the next room? Or worse, down here having dinner. Eww. It's awkward."

Simon chuckled, finally glancing up at her, the glint of mischief in his eyes a contrast to the underlying tension. "We'll just keep things quiet."

Angie's face flushed a deep shade of pink, and she swatted at him playfully, though her embarrassment was real. "Not funny," she mumbled, trying to hide her flustered state behind the pile of invitations.

For a moment, there was silence between them, but it was a silence loaded with unspoken things. Angie's mind drifted back to the engagement photo session, the one that had left a sour taste in her mouth. She had been trying to avoid the topic, but it gnawed at her, refusing to stay buried.

She took a deep breath, her voice quieter now. "We haven't talked about the engagement pictures."

Simon's brow furrowed slightly as he glanced up again. "What about 'em?"

Angie hesitated, feeling her frustration begin to bubble to the surface again. "Well, you were... I don't know, lit."

Simon's face hardened almost imperceptibly, and she saw the shift in his demeanor. He didn't want to talk about this. "What about it?" he asked, his tone clipped.

Angie felt the familiar sting of disappointment, her chest tightening as she pushed forward. "What happened?" she asked, her voice rising slightly with the tension. "That whole thing was awful."

Simon's movements became rougher, more mechanical, as he stuffed another envelope into the pile. "Well," he said tersely, "I took pills on an empty stomach. Lesson learned."

Angie stared at him, her frustration mounting. *That's it?* She couldn't believe how casually he was brushing it off, as if it hadn't been a big deal, as if it hadn't broken something fragile between them. "That's it?" she pressed, her voice cracking slightly.

"Pretty much," Simon replied, his voice flat.

The kettle on the stove began to whistle, the high-pitched sound cutting through the thick tension between them. Angie stood abruptly, her emotions teetering on the edge. She moved to the stove, her hands shaking slightly as she reached for the kettle. "So what?" she snapped, her voice sharp with frustration. "Now you'll have a fuckin' Pop Tart before you pop any pills?"

Simon's response was flippant, dismissive. "Sure. With frosting."

The words stung, but what hurt more was the lack of seriousness in his tone, the way he seemed to shrug off everything that had been weighing on her heart. She turned to face him, her anger boiling over. "Simon."

He barely glanced up at her, his attention on the kettle. "The kettle."

Angie's frustration reached its peak. She grabbed the kettle, swinging it off the stove with more force than she intended. The movement was quick, careless, and in an instant, one of the delicate tea cups on the counter was knocked to the floor. It shattered with a sharp crash, pieces of porcelain scattering across the kitchen tiles.

Angie froze, her breath catching in her throat. "Your mom's tea cup," she whispered, guilt washing over her in waves. It was one of Susan's favorite pieces, and now it lay broken, just like everything else.

Simon shook his head, chuckling as if the situation hadn't just escalated. "You're gonna be grounded," he teased.

Angie knelt down, her hands trembling as she reached for the broken pieces. The engagement photos, the pills, and the pressure of the wedding all made it hard to breathe. She felt like she was coming apart at the seams.

Simon joined her on the floor, gently taking her hand in his. His touch was warm, grounding her in the moment, but it did little to ease the ache in her chest. "Hey," he said, his voice gentle now. "It's not a big deal, okay? I'm fine."

Angie wanted to believe him, but the cracks between them were growing wider, and she didn't know how to fix them. She melted slightly under his touch, letting herself lean into him for a moment. His presence was comforting, but it wasn't enough to chase away the doubts that lingered in the back of her mind.

Simon leaned in, kissing her. For a moment, everything else faded away, and it was just the two of them, wrapped in the fragile warmth of their connection. He moved to lift her onto the counter, his hands slipping around her waist in a playful gesture, but Angie shook her head, gently pushing him away.

"Nope," she said, her voice playful but firm. "Not in your parents' kitchen."

Simon groaned, rolling his eyes in mock frustration. "Man, why you gotta sizzle out my heat?"

Angie smiled faintly, but it didn't reach her eyes. The playful banter was a temporary distraction, but it couldn't cover up the deeper cracks that were beginning to show. The tea cup wasn't the only thing that was broken.

Six

Dancing Between the Raindrops

The air buzzed with excitement and anticipation. Angie stood at the back of the church, her heart fluttering with a mix of nerves and joy as she adjusted her mantilla veil for the tenth time. Everything felt surreal. This was the day she had dreamed of, the day she would walk down the aisle to marry Simon. The love of her life, her best friend. The unease she had felt in the days leading up to the wedding seemed to fade into the background, replaced by the dizzying excitement of the moment.

She clutched her bouquet tightly, the delicate calla lilies trembling slightly in her grip. Her father, Edgar, stood beside her, his eyes filled with pride and a hint of tears. He offered her his arm, and she took it, feeling the warmth of his love and support grounding her as they prepared to make the walk down the aisle.

Simon straightened his suit jacket. Jared, ever the jokester, gave him a playful punch on the arm, teasing him about finally settling down. Simon laughed it off, but his eyes held a seriousness that Jared hadn't seen before. This was real, Simon thought. He was about to become a husband, and while the gravity of it hadn't fully hit him, he knew today marked the beginning of something new, something bigger than either of them.

The music began to swell, and the doors opened. Angie's breath caught in her throat as she stepped forward, the church illuminated by the golden light streaming through the stained glass windows. The pews were filled with their closest family and friends, faces glowing with smiles and teary eyes. But Angie's gaze was fixed solely on Simon, waiting for her at the altar.

Angie's heart raced as she clung to her father's arm, walking down the aisle with slow, deliberate steps. The world seemed to narrow to a single point. Simon, standing at the altar, waiting for her.

He looked more handsome than ever in his pinstripe suit, his broad shoulders straight, his eyes locked on her. For a brief moment, Angie's heart swelled so much she thought it might burst. *He's mine*, she thought with a giddy sense of disbelief. *We're really doing this.*

As she reached the altar, tears glistened in her father's eyes as he kissed her cheek, gently placing her hand in Simon's. His touch gentle and reassuring. There was a tenderness in the exchange that made Angie's throat tighten. She blinked away her own tears, overwhelmed by the beauty of it all. The air was filled with love, the scent of the flowers from her bouquet, the glow of the candles flickering in the dim light of the church.

The world around them seemed to blur, and all Angie could focus on was the warmth of his hands in hers, the steady rhythm of his breath, and the love shining in his eyes. For this moment, everything was perfect. Every doubt, every worry she'd ever had, seemed insignificant compared to the joy she felt standing here with him.

The priest's voice was steady as he led them through their vows. Angie listened, her heart fluttering as Simon spoke his words, clear and confident:

"I, Simon, take you, Angelina, for my lawful wife, to have and to hold, from this day forward..."

As he spoke, Angie's mind filled with the happy memories they had shared. The late-night phone calls, surprise dates, the way he made her laugh when she didn't think she could, and the way he held her when everything felt too overwhelming. This was what love was, she told herself.

When it was her turn to speak, Angie's voice trembled slightly with emotion, but there was no hesitation in her heart.

"For richer, for poorer, in sickness and in health, until death do us part."

The words felt like a promise she could believe in, a future she could almost taste. It was wide open, and all she could see was the life they would build together.

Hand in hand, Angie and Simon walked down the aisle as husband and wife, the cheers of their guests ringing in their ears. Angie's heart soared as she clung to Simon's arm, her cheeks aching from the smile that hadn't left her face since the ceremony had begun. She was a wife now. *His* wife. It felt almost too good to be true.

They moved through the day in a blur of laughter and congratulations, posing for family pictures outside the church, the sun casting a warm glow over everything. Angie's dress sparkled in the light, the delicate lace catching the rays as she leaned into Simon, her arm looped through his.

The small outdoor reception was exactly as Angie had imagined it with twinkling fairy lights strung between the trees, tables draped in white linens, and a simple but beautiful cake in the center. Their friends and family mingled, glasses clinking, voices full of warmth and celebration. Angie and Simon swayed together for their first dance, his arms wrapped securely around her waist, pulling her close as the music played.

As they danced under the glow of the lights, Angie felt like the world had paused just for them. There were no worries, no fears, only the rhythm of the music and the steady beat of Simon's heart against hers. For the first time in what felt like forever, Angie allowed herself to believe in the perfect happiness of the moment. The future was bright, filled with endless possibilities, and in Simon's arms, she felt invincible.

Nothing could touch them today.

Seven

Bracing for Impact

A few weeks after the wedding, the glow of newlywed bliss had started to fade, and the reality of day-to-day life was settling in. The thrill of the wedding day was replaced by the rhythm of bills, work, and the growing discomfort of cramped space in the in-law quarters. Simon and Angie had dreamed of starting their life together, but no one had warned them how quickly the mundane would take over. There was no time for long, lazy mornings or spontaneous adventures. It was all about surviving, finding a way to make it all work.

The office life buzzed around Angie as she sat in her cubicle, staring blankly at the screen. The familiar *Hollister Aircraft* logo flickered as her screen saver, a steady reminder of the job she was tethered to. But today, her mind wasn't on work. It was far from the numbers, the orders for bolt and screws, the humdrum routine of the day.

Her fingers absentmindedly traced the edges of the wedding photo frame perched on her desk. The date inscribed below the image—February 12th, 2005—seemed to glow with nostalgia that only deepened her current frustration. In the picture, she and Simon looked perfect. Smiling. Happy. Her dress shimmering in the light, his arm wrapped protectively around her waist. They were the image of what love was supposed to look like. But as Angie cradled the phone receiver in one hand, her other hand pressed against her temple, the present moment felt crushing.

"This is not okay, Simon," she said, trying to keep her voice even, but the frustration seeped through, sharp at the edges. Her eyes narrowed at nothing in particular, her thoughts swirling around the conversation.

Simon's voice, though inaudible from this side of the receiver, had a tone she knew too well; dismissive, deflective, brushing her concerns aside like dust on the wind. She let out a slow breath, trying not to snap.

"You can't keep spending money like this," Angie continued, her voice tightening as her emotions bubbled closer to the surface. "It's... it's a lot."

She could hear his response, something half-hearted and defensive, but it didn't soothe her. Nothing about this situation felt right. She knew something was wrong, but she felt stuck, trapped between wanting to fix it and knowing she couldn't control what was happening. The helplessness gnawed at her.

"Fine," she muttered, pressing her lips together. It wasn't fine. Not at all. But she was too tired to argue any further.

"Um-hm," Angie mumbled, her fingers gripping the phone tightly. "K, thank you." The words felt hollow, an empty formality.

With a sigh, she hung up the phone and stared at the empty office around her. The stillness of the room made her feel even more isolated. The tightness in her chest grew as frustration welled up inside her. Before she could stop herself, Angie grabbed a small post-it pad from the desk and bit down on it, muffling a scream of pure exasperation. Her body tensed as she jumped up from her chair and wildly punched the air, throwing her frustration into the space around her.

And then she froze.

A tap on the cubicle wall startled her, and she turned to see Benjamin, one of her older colleagues, standing there with a bemused but kind expression. His thinning hair and gentle eyes gave him a fatherly vibe that always made Angie feel a little sheepish when caught like this.

"Uh, Angelina?" Benjamin's voice was gentle, his words carefully neutral. "Any more orders for the morning? UPS will be here in about 20 minutes."

Angie quickly smoothed down her shirt, trying to regain her composure. "Nope, uh yeah," she stammered, reaching for a file on her desk. "Hold on. One more."

Benjamin nodded, giving her a small smile before disappearing back into his own workspace. Angie exhaled slowly, sinking back into her chair. The post-it note pad sat crumpled on the desk in front of her, a sad little symbol of how off-track things had become. She wasn't sure how much longer she could keep pretending everything was fine.

Outside, the afternoon sun cast a glow on the loading dock, its warmth contrasting with the storm swirling inside Angie's mind. She and Erica sat side by side, eating their lunches in the familiar quiet of long-time friends. Erica, older and wiser, had seen Angie through plenty of ups and downs. Her calm presence was the balm Angie needed right now, even if she didn't know how to fix things.

Angie picked at her sandwich, her mind still stuck on her conversation with Simon earlier. "Am I making too much of it?" she asked, her voice barely above a whisper.

Erica glanced over, her eyes thoughtful as she took a bite of her salad. "I don't think so," she replied after a moment. "Could it be a phase?"

Angie sighed, leaning back against the wall of the building. "Yeah, or maybe I'm scared it's a problem."

Erica nodded, her gaze turning to the horizon, lost in thought. "Yeah, I can see that."

Angie's fingers fidgeting with the edge of her lunch bag. "Then I'll want to fix it. Can I fix it?"

Erica looked at Angie. "I don't think so," she said gently. "I think it's more like... you have to figure out what you are to the problem."

Angie's brow furrowed, confusion knitting her thoughts together. "What does that mean?" she asked, her voice tinged with frustration.

"You know," Erica said, her voice calm but pointed, "like, are you part of the problem?"

Angie bristled, sitting up a little straighter. "Why am I the problem?" she asked defensively. "I'm just trying to help him."

Erica shrugged. "I know, I'm just talking out loud here."

Angie's shoulders slumped as she let out a tired breath. "I see him in pain, but... is he managing it properly? I don't know."

Erica nodded, her tone more serious now. "Right, like is he supposed to blow your savings to support the 'neighborhood pharmacist'?"

Angie let out a bitter laugh, shaking her head. "His mom is the problem. He can't even fart without her thinking he's dying."

Erica raised an eyebrow, her lips quirking into a half-smile. "Maybe because she sees the train coming down a busted-ass track."

Angie blinked, caught off guard. "What?"

Erica leaned forward, her voice low and steady. "You know, like... it's probably not the first time the rails got loose. She's probably seen more than you think."

Angie stared at her, absorbing the words. She wanted to dismiss them, but deep down, she knew Erica was probably right. Simon's mom had always been overly protective, but maybe it wasn't just paranoia. Maybe there was something darker beneath it all, something Angie hadn't fully seen before.

"You talk like you're Obi-Wan or something," Angie said, trying to lighten the moment, though her thoughts were still tangled in the seriousness of their conversation.

Erica chuckled. "It's Yoda."

"Whatever. Yoda," Angie muttered, but a faint smile tugged at her lips.

They sat in silence for a moment, their conversation lingering in the air. Angie's heart aching and her mind spinning with questions she didn't have the answers to. She loved Simon, but the cracks in their relationship were growing wider, and she wasn't sure how to keep them from breaking apart completely.

Eight

On the Prowl

The night air was crisp, and the faint thump of music could be heard long before Angie and Simon reached the house. Cars lined both sides of the street, a clear sign that the house party was already in full swing. Angie walked beside Simon, her hand nervously wrapped around his arm as they made their way up the driveway to a modest, mid-class home. The music grew louder with every step, the bass vibrating through the ground beneath her feet.

"I always feel weird being here," Angie muttered, glancing around at the people who loitered outside, red plastic cups in hand.

Simon shot her a reassuring smile, squeezing her hand gently. "Why? You know these people."

"Yeah, but..." Angie hesitated, biting her lip as they reached the door. "It's like a den of wolves."

Simon stopped, raising an eyebrow at her, amused. "What?"

Angie shrugged, trying to explain the unease that had settled in her chest. "You guys travel in a pack, it's a little intimidating. And you throw in the drinking and *stuff...*" She trailed off, glancing at the door as a cloud of smoke wafted out. "A girl's gotta come strapped."

Simon chuckled, shaking his head. "Stay close, sugar. I got you."

With a playful grin, he led her through the front door and into the thick haze of pot smoke that greeted them. The house was packed, bodies pressing together in the crowded space. The living room was filled with a mishmash of furniture: an old pool table stood in the center, surrounded by folding chairs and a large comfy sofa that had seen better days. A giant fish tank bubbled in the corner, the glow from the tank illuminating the faces of people playing darts nearby.

Angie clung to Simon's side as they made their way toward the kitchen, where his friends would undoubtedly be. She never felt fully comfortable in these situations, there was always an underlying current of chaos that made her uneasy, but she tried her best to push it aside. *Simon has your back*, she reminded herself.

As they reached the kitchen, Simon let out a loud whoop, his voice rising above the music. "Whooty whoo, motherfuckers!"

Fish, one of Simon's lankier friends with an elaborate koi tattoo covering his back, turned with a grin. He was standing with Johnny, another of Simon's buddies, who greeted them with a raised beer.

"What up, Scrill?" Fish said with a nod and a handshake, flashing Angie a friendly smile. "Hey, Ang."

"Hey, Fish," Angie replied, her voice barely audible over the noise.

"The big balla' finally rolled in," Johnny teased, giving Simon a playful punch on the arm.

Simon laughed, his energy matching the vibe of the room. "Hey man, a little business before pleasure. What you got on the menu, homie?"

Fish raised an eyebrow, his grin widening. "Magic beans, baby."

"Well shit, man, hook da brothers up," Simon said, his eyes gleaming.

Fish motioned for them to follow him as they made their way through the crowded house toward a back room. Angie trailed behind, her stomach churning slightly with unease. She knew what was coming, and every fiber of her being told her she didn't want to be a part of it. But she kept quiet, staying close to Simon, hoping this would all blow over quickly.

Fish led them to a door at the back of the house, knocking with a series of taps. A moment later, Freddy, mid-thirties and already looking out of it, cracked the door open with the chain still in place.

"What's the password?" Freddy asked, his voice slurred with amusement.

Fish didn't miss a beat. "Your ex-hyna was great last night."

Freddy's grin faltered, but he unlocked the door, shaking his head. "Shit, why so close to home, man?"

"You asked, homie," Fish replied with a shrug.

Freddy laughed it off, stepping aside to let them in. The room was dimly lit, cluttered with mismatched furniture and the distinct smell of something stronger than pot. Freddy, already finishing up a line of coke, danced out of the room with exaggerated steps, shouting over his shoulder. "Woo wee, they be playin' my song. Make way, homies. I'ma 'bout to groove these kicks."

As Freddy disappeared, Fish led them to a striped brown and yellow couch from the 70s. Simon and Johnny immediately took a seat, while Angie remained standing in the corner, arms wrapped around herself. She tried to act like she didn't care about what was happening, but inside, her discomfort was growing by the second.

Fish moved toward the closet and slid open the doors, revealing a large safe. Inside were several large pill containers, each marked with their original pharmaceutical labels. For a moment, he looked like some twisted version of a pharmacist, meticulously surveying his inventory and preparing to fill a prescription only without a white coat and ethics.

"What do you need?" Fish asked, pulling out a variety of bottles.

Johnny leaned forward, pulling out some cash. "I got about one-twenty. Give me some bars and a few sleepers."

Simon, never one to be outdone, leaned back casually. "Give me one fifty in Norcos, fifty in bars, and then some Somas and Valiums sprinkled in."

Fish smiled, reaching deeper into the safe. "Here, these are a nice surprise," he said, handing Simon and Johnny a couple of 80mg Oxycontin.

Angie's heart raced. She didn't know where to look, her eyes darting around the room as if she could somehow escape witnessing the transaction. *Why am I even here?* she thought. *I don't belong in this world.*

"These just came in," Fish continued, clearly proud of his stash. "If you like 'em, they're twenty bucks a pop."

Johnny groaned. "Fuck. Twenty?"

"Oxycontin," Fish said with a grin. "Worth every penny, my friend."

Fish then pulled out a box of Fentanyl pops. Angie's breath caught in her throat. She didn't know much about drugs, but she knew enough to realize this wasn't just casual partying anymore.

"Damn, Fish, what are those?" Simon asked, his eyes widening.

"These are the bomb-diggety," Fish replied, his tone playful. "Make all your dreams come true."

Angie felt like the walls were closing in. Her jaw dropped as she watched Simon and Johnny casually toss money at Fish, joking about the pills as if they were trading candy. Simon took the Fentanyl pops without hesitation, his voice light as he joked, "Double D strip tease, here I come."

Fish laughed, doling out pills like candy. "Go easy on that new shit. They give it to dying cancer patients."

Angie's mind swirled. *Dying cancer patients?* Her hands trembled, and she clenched them into fists, trying to keep calm, but it was becoming harder to ignore the pit forming in her stomach.

As the banter between Simon and Johnny continued, Angie forced herself to stay quiet, biting her lip to keep from saying anything that might embarrass Simon. But inside, she was screaming. *How do you even get that shit?*

Nine

Everything's Temporary

Angie came home from work, her mind still spinning from what she had witnessed at the party over the weekend. She stepped into the bedroom she shared with Simon, immediately spotting his mother, Susan, standing by his nightstand, folding laundry.

"Hi, Angie," Susan said with her usual forced cheerfulness. "Sorry, I was just stacking the clean laundry here."

Angie forced a tight smile, trying to push aside her lingering frustration. "Thank you, but you don't have to do that. I can do the laundry."

Susan waved her off. "Oh, don't be silly. It's better to make full loads than have to do little ones. I don't mind, really."

Angie felt her cheeks flush with embarrassment as Susan handed her a pile of her folded underwear. "Thank you," she muttered, awkwardly.

Susan wasn't done. "So, do you know if Simon's gone to the doctor recently?" she asked, her voice tinged with concern.

Angie blinked, caught off guard by the question. "I don't think he has," she replied, unsure of where this conversation was heading.

Downstairs, the sound of the front door opening echoed through the house, followed by Simon's cheerful whistling.

Susan leaned in slightly, lowering her voice. "Do you know if he's gotten pills from his friends?"

Angie's heart skipped a beat. "Um, his friends do pills?" she asked, feigning ignorance. "I don't really know."

"I'm pretty sure they share them or something like that," Susan continued, her voice matter-of-fact. "I'm not one hundred percent positive."

Angie's mind racing. Before she could say anything more, Susan gave her a tight smile and exited the room, moving to corner Simon at the top of the stairs.

The hallway outside their bedroom was thick with tension. Angie stood just out of view, leaning against the doorframe as she listened to Simon and his mother, Susan, exchange pleasantries. Her hands fidgeted with the fabric of her shirt, but her ears were tuned in to every word.

"I just put your clean clothes on your bed, Simon dear," Susan said, her voice syrupy with the forced sweetness that Angie had come to expect.

"Thanks, Ma," Simon replied, his voice casual. Too casual.

Angie held her breath as the conversation shifted to more uncomfortable territory. She knew what was coming. It was always the same when Susan cornered Simon like this. There was no escaping her questions.

"Have you seen Dr. Takeda recently?" Susan asked, her voice taking on that familiar note of concern.

"No, I have to make an appointment soon," Simon replied, but Angie could hear the impatience creeping into his tone. He never liked answering these kinds of questions, especially when the truth was something he didn't want to admit.

Susan didn't miss a beat. "So how'd you get those pills?" Her voice was calm, but the question hung in the air.

Angie froze, her stomach tightening. She had hoped that maybe Susan wouldn't notice, that maybe they could avoid this confrontation. But, of course, she had seen the pills. Susan missed nothing.

"What pills?" Simon's voice was suddenly defensive, and Angie could picture him, hands in his pockets, trying to play it cool.

"The ones I just saw in your nightstand," Susan said, her words cutting through the air like a knife.

Simon paused for a moment before offering a half-hearted explanation. "From a different doctor."

Susan wasn't buying it. "Who?"

Simon's voice was sharper now. "What difference does it make? My back hurts, and I need something."

Susan's sigh was audible, the kind that carried years of exasperation. "You need to be honest with me, son."

Angie's jaw clenched as she stood just inside the bedroom, her heart pounding. This wasn't going to end well. Simon never liked being questioned like this, especially by his mother.

"Fine. I got them from a friend," Simon admitted, his voice low.

"You can't be doing that," Susan said firmly.

"You're right. I probably shouldn't." Simon's words were dismissive, his tone almost flippant.

Susan wasn't done yet. "Does your wife know all this?"

Angie's breath hitched, her eyes narrowing. *Here we go*, she thought, her frustration building.

"She probably does," Simon muttered, clearly trying to end the conversation.

"Well, please tell her she needs to be honest with me too," Susan added, her voice dripping with that familiar tone of control.

That was it. Angie had heard enough. She stepped out of the bedroom, her eyes locked on Susan. "Um, I don't think I answer to you," she said, her voice tight with barely restrained anger.

Susan turned to face her, unfazed. "You are living in my house, though," she replied, her tone calm but laced with subtle superiority.

Angie bristled. "And I appreciate that, but it's not by my choice."

Susan's lips tightened into a thin smile. "Simon, you know how we do things in this house. Honesty is a cornerstone... not that everyone grows up with it. Please respect it." She turned to walk away, but not before adding, "Dinner will be ready shortly."

The tension in the air was thick as Angie and Simon stood there, watching Susan retreat down the hallway.

"Okay," Simon said, his voice resigned.

"No thank you," Angie said at the same time, her words sharp. "We're headed to my mom's."

Susan paused for a moment, her voice floating back over her shoulder. "Simon, please give me adequate notice if you won't be here for dinner. Thank you."

The sound of Susan's footsteps disappeared down the stairs, and Angie's fists unclenched. She could barely contain the frustration bubbling inside her. Before Simon could say anything, she grabbed his arm and pulled him into their cramped bedroom, shutting the door behind them with a snap.

"What the hell, Si?" Angie hissed, her eyes blazing as she turned to face him.

Simon leaned against the door, his hands in his pockets, his expression calm, almost bored. "Don't worry about it," he said with a shrug. "She worries for no reason. Just blow it off."

Angie stared at him, her frustration reaching a boiling point. "I can't!" she snapped, her voice rising. "I'm new here. We're supposed to be baking cookies together and shit, but instead, I'm disrespectful to her in her house!"

Simon raised his hands, trying to calm her down. "Girl, you need to tone down that jam."

Angie felt like she was going to explode. "*This* is not working," she said, her voice shaking with emotion. "I'm playing a loyalty game here that I don't want to. I don't want to live here anymore, Simon."

Simon sighed, running a hand through his hair. "And we're not going to. We're saving up for a place."

Angie scoffed, her arms crossing over her chest. "You know how much we've saved up? Five hundred bucks. What the hell are we supposed to do with that, buy a front door?"

Simon stepped closer to her, his easy tone tried to diffuse the situation. "So it's taking a little longer," he said, his hands gently resting on her arms.

Angie's eyes narrowed as she glared at him. "And you keep spending money on those dumb cock pills," she shot back, her voice filled with frustration.

Simon sighed, pulling her closer. "Baby, I need them," he murmured, his voice low. "You don't know what it's like to be in this kind of pain. I can't sit on my ass without hurting. All day long, I'm in pain."

Angie's anger wavered for a moment as Simon's words sank in, but the frustration remained. "How much longer?" she asked, her voice quieter now. "Six months? Five years?"

Simon pressed his lips to her neck, his hands moving to her waist. "Six months," he whispered against her skin. "It'll be okay."

For a moment, Angie felt herself thawing under his touch, her resolve weakening. But then reality came crashing back, and she pulled away from him, shaking her head. "I'm serious, Simon," she said firmly. "Six months."

Simon's smile faltered for a moment, but he nodded, trying to reassure her. "Six months," he repeated, his voice steady, as he kissed her neck.

Damn him. But Angie wasn't sure she could wait that long.

TEN

DOWN AND OUT

The kitchen of Angie's childhood home had always been a place of warmth and comfort. The modest space, with its simple decor and well-worn furniture, had been the heart of her childhood. Now, as she sat at the small table, with a pot of her mother's homemade albondigas soup steaming in the center, that comfort seemed to slip away, replaced by a growing sense of unease.

Across from her, Simon sat with his head drooping lower and lower over his plate, his eyes barely open. Angie glanced at her mother, Sofia, who sat beside her, watching Simon intently. The concern on Sofia's face mirrored the knot tightening in Angie's stomach.

The kitchen, with its colorful Diego Rivera painting, *The Flower Carrier*, and the old portrayal of *The Last Supper* hanging on the wall, seemed to close in around them. The once-familiar setting now felt foreign, overshadowed by the tension in the air.

"This is not normal," Sofia said quietly, her voice low but firm. Her eyes shifted from Simon back to Angie, filled with the kind of maternal wisdom Angie had come to depend on.

Angie sighed, her shoulders slumping. "It's that medication he takes," she replied, trying to keep her voice even, though inside, the frustration and fear were mounting.

Sofia frowned, her eyes narrowing. "*Mijo! Simon!*" she called out, her tone sharper now.

Simon barely reacted, his head lolling to one side as he struggled to open his eyes. It was as if the effort to stay awake was too much for him, his body full of exhaustion or something more insidious.

Angie's heart hurt as she looked at him. "Can he lie down in my old room?" she asked, turning to her mother.

"Of course," Sofia said, her voice filled with concern. She knew what this moment meant, even if Angie wasn't fully ready to accept it yet.

Angie stood and moved to Simon's side, gently taking his arm. "Come on, Simon," she said, her voice tender but firm. "Go lie down."

Simon stood slowly, his movements sluggish and uncoordinated. Angie guided him down the narrow hallway, upstairs to her old bedroom, the room that still held pieces of her past: photos on the wall, a few books scattered on the shelves. The beds were still neatly made, just as her mother always kept it, and as Simon collapsed onto the mattress, his feet dangling over the edge, Angie's heart clenched.

She knelt down, carefully removing his shoes. As she looked at him, her eyes teared up. He smiled at her, a silly grin spreading across his face, as though he didn't have a care in the world. But Angie knew better. The man she loved was drifting further away, and she wasn't sure how to pull him back.

Simon's eyes fluttered shut, and within moments, he was asleep. Angie stood there for a long moment, watching him, the tears that had been building finally spilling over. She wiped them away quickly, pulling herself together before heading back to the kitchen.

When Angie returned to the table, Sofia was still seated, her hands resting in her lap, her expression thoughtful. Angie sat down across from her, the situation pressing down on her shoulders like a heavy blanket.

"Trouble in honeymoon land?" Sofia asked gently..

Angie let out a nervous laugh, shaking her head. "Ha, I don't think we ever got there, Ma."

Sofia raised an eyebrow, her eyes serious. "What's going on?"

Angie took a deep breath, her fingers nervously tracing the edge of her soup bowl. These were hard words to say. Words she had been avoiding, but ones that now demanded to be spoken. "Well... besides butting heads with his mom, I think he's hooked on those pain meds. I mean, he *is, Simon is addicted to pain pills*," she admitted, her voice breaking slightly as the reality of it hit her again.

Sofia's brow furrowed in concern. "*Ay, Mija*," she murmured, reaching across the table to take Angie's hand.

Angie squeezed her mother's hand, grateful for the comfort but still feeling lost. "Since his accident... what, three years ago? He's been on meds, but now it's different."

Sofia nodded, her expression knowing. "Well, yeah, you're married now."

Angie sighed, shaking her head. "No... yes, but it's more than that. It's all just... more. I don't know what it means. I'm just scared, Ma."

Sofia's eyes saddened even more, her face filled with understanding. "Did you think he was magically going to stop?"

Angie hesitated, her throat tight. "No," she whispered, "I don't think I thought of it as a problem."

Sofia let out a sigh, her gaze holding Angie's firmly. "So now it is, and it means you're married to someone who's sick."

The words hit Angie like a punch to the gut, but she knew they were true. She had seen the signs, but she had ignored them, hoping it would all somehow fix itself. Now, that hope felt foolish.

"I know," Angie said quietly, her voice barely above a whisper. "I guess it's my fault for ignoring the signs."

Sofia shook her head, her expression thoughtful. "Mijita, we pray for signs, and then we tell them what they mean. That's backward." She paused, her voice firm. "We should find direction from the inside out. Pray, Not for the answers but for strength. You need to know that this kind of sickness... it's ugly. My grandfather was a drunk. I remember the ugly." Sofia's eyes filled with memories, distant but still painful. "And you're a newlywed."

Angie nodded, wiping at her eyes. "I know, I know, Ma," she said, her voice trembling. "I love him, and I need to help care for him."

Sofia leaned forward, her gaze sharp. "*No, Mija*," she said firmly. "With this, it will test your commitment to him. It's going to test *you*. You love him, sure, but is it like, I don't know, Frida and Diego?"

Angie's eyes widened, her heart sinking. "Ma, they were crazy," she said, trying to laugh it off, but the seriousness of the conversation weighed heavily on her.

Sofia smiled. "I know, but fierce in love. *Entiendes?*"

Angie nodded. "*Sí*. Love him till my wheels fall off," she whispered, though the words felt heavier than they ever had before.

Sofia nodded, her eyes filled with love and understanding. "Exactly, *Mija*. But don't forget, you need to take care of yourself, too."

ELEVEN

SEASONS OF NO CHANGE

The seasons passed, summer's heat had given way to the cool winds of fall, and now, the chill of winter had descended, bringing with it the hustle and bustle of the holiday season. But for Angie, the change in weather did little to shift the growing tension in their lives.

Christmas decorations filled the car bay of *Blazin' Audio*, garlands and twinkling lights draped across the walls in an attempt to bring cheer to the industrial space. But Simon wasn't feeling festive. His body ached, each movement sharp with pain that radiated from his lower back, seizing up every time he tried to stretch or bend. He was crammed inside the tight space of a customer's sedan, installing an audio system, but his focus kept slipping away, lost in the haze of discomfort.

Grimacing, Simon leaned back, breathing deeply to try to push through the pain, but it wasn't working. His body screamed for relief. With a resigned sigh, he pulled out his Nokia, flipping it open with stiff fingers and dialing quickly.

"Hey, man," he said, his voice low, trying to mask the desperation in his tone. "You got time for a house call? Yeah. Work. Late."

He hung up, rubbing his temples as he leaned back against the car seat, eyes closed for a moment. The holiday decorations twinkled around him, but all Simon could think about was numbing the pain, just for a little while. *Just until I can breathe again*, he thought, the familiar justification echoing in his mind.

Later that afternoon, the sound of a rumbling engine echoed through the car bay as Fish pulled up in his pristine '66 Lincoln Continental. The sleek car glided to a stop, and Simon straightened up, wincing slightly as he stood. He walked over to the passenger side and slipped into the seat, the smell of leather and cigarette smoke greeting him.

Fish grinned, his eyes hidden behind dark sunglasses. "One of those days, huh, man?" he asked, glancing over at Simon as he slumped into the seat.

Simon ran a hand through his hair, shaking his head. "Non-stop. I feel like a fuckin' pussy. Every move hurts."

Fish nodded knowingly, reaching into his pocket. "I know, man. Here."

With a flick of his wrist, Fish handed Simon a handful of Oxycontin. The small white pills glistened in the dim light of the car bay, and Simon didn't hesitate, pulling out a handful of twenties in exchange. It was routine by now, the kind of transaction that had become as normal as a handshake.

But before Simon could pocket the pills, Freddy popped up from the back seat with a wide grin.

"What the hell, Freddy!" Simon exclaimed, startled.

Freddy chuckled, leaning forward with his arms draped over the back of the seat. "What up, meyn? I'm his assistant today."

Fish laughed, shaking his head. "His old lady kicked him out again."

Simon smirked, pocketing the pills. "You and your crazy broads, man."

"I know, I know," Freddy said with a dramatic sigh. Then, as if remembering something important, he fished around in his jacket and pulled out a small patch. "Hey, boss, I got a patch he could preview."

Freddy handed the patch to Simon, his grin widening. Fish nodded in approval. "Good call, Mr. Assistant. Fentanyl in a patch. Like those pops, but a slower release into your system."

Simon raised an eyebrow, examining the patch in his hand. "How many buffalos?" he asked, already knowing it wouldn't be cheap.

"Sixty," Fish replied, his grin never faltering. "But for you? Fifty."

Simon whistled low. "Each, dang, man. Alright, just one."

He pocketed the patch, feeling the familiar tug of temptation as the price echoed in his mind. But before he could say anything more, he opened the car door, stepping out into the cool winter air. "Assistant?" he called back, shaking his head with a wry smile.

Fish smirked, leaning back in his seat. "I'd be like you with a nine to five if it wasn't for my lawyer."

"That doesn't make me feel better," Simon shot back, closing the car door behind him.

Fish chuckled. "It makes me feel better," he said, revving the engine.

"Dick," Simon muttered under his breath as the car peeled away, leaving him standing alone in the fading daylight, his pockets full but his soul heavy.

Twelve

Still Standing (Somehow)

In the very early morning that followed, in the dim light of the Wagner bedroom, Angie lay asleep, her body curled under the warmth of the blankets. But Simon wasn't beside her. He was fumbling around the room, his movements exaggerated and clumsy. His eyes drooped, his speech slurred, and his body swayed with every step.

Angie stirred, blinking in the darkness as she heard him moving around. "What's wrong?" she asked groggily, her voice thick with sleep.

Simon mumbled something, still searching the room. "Sorry," he slurred, his words barely coherent.

Angie sat up slightly, rubbing her eyes as she tried to make sense of what was happening. "What are you doing?" she asked, her voice more alert now.

"I'm looking for my beans," Simon muttered, his hands rifling through drawers. "I lost them."

Angie frowned, her heart sinking as she realized what he meant. "You lost them, or did you take them?" she asked, her voice tinged with frustration.

"More," Simon mumbled, still searching. "I had more."

Angie's eyes flicked to the bed, where several prescription bottles lay scattered across the rumpled sheets. The sight of them made her angry. His addiction, the storm cloud that never cleared.

"Simon, go back to sleep," she said, trying to keep her voice steady.

But Simon wasn't listening. He was restless, pacing the small room with unsteady steps. "I need a walk," he muttered. "I need to think about things."

Angie sighed, half-asleep but too concerned to ignore him. She glanced out the window, the darkness of the night reflected back at her. "Bad idea, babe," she said, her voice gentle but firm. "You can't even stand up to piss."

Simon ignored her, his frustration bubbling to the surface. "I don't need this," he muttered, his words slurring together.

Angie rubbed her face, exhaustion tugging at her, but the worry gnawing at her wouldn't let her rest. She glanced back out the window, the rain pattering softly against the glass. "Calm down," she said, her voice barely above a whisper. "Look, see? It's totally dark out, and it's raining. You'll get lost and fall asleep on the curb."

For a moment, Simon stalled, his body swaying like a leaning tower ready to collapse. Angie watched him, concerned, but she was too drained to fight him. Slowly, Simon's body gave in, his eyelids drooping as he dozed off where he stood.

Angie lay back down, pulling the blanket up around her shoulders, her eyes staring blankly at the ceiling. And as the rain continued to fall, the future felt more uncertain than ever.

Thirteen

Breaking Dawn

The early morning air was still and cool, the faint light of dawn beginning to creep through the windows. Angie stirred in bed, sleep clinging to her as she slowly opened her eyes. For a moment, everything seemed calm, the stillness of the house lulling her into a false sense of security. But then, she realized—Simon was gone.

Her heart skipped a beat as she sat up, her eyes scanning the room frantically. The empty space next to her felt like a gaping hole, and a wave of dread crashed over her.

"Simon?" she called into the darkness, but there was no answer. Panic surged through her as she threw off the blankets and jumped out of bed, her bare feet hitting the cold floor with a thud. She didn't bother with shoes or a jacket, her hands fumbling to pull on her jeans as she rushed toward the bedroom door.

The house was eerily quiet as Angie moved quickly through the rooms, her eyes darting around in search of any sign of Simon. She checked the office, the hallway, and the bathroom. Nothing. Her breath quickened as she moved downstairs, her footsteps echoing in the empty spaces.

"Simon!" she called out again, her voice rising with fear. She searched the living room, the kitchen, even the small storage closet under the stairs. But Simon was nowhere to be found.

Her heart pounded in her chest as the realization set in. *He's gone.*

"Shit," she muttered under her breath, the knot of fear tightening in her stomach.

Without thinking, she rushed toward the front door, her mind racing with possibilities. *Where could he have gone?* She threw open the door, the cold air hitting her like a slap to the face, but she barely felt it.

Outside, the world was hushed, the light beginning to break over the horizon. A faint drizzle hung in the air, clinging to everything it touched and making the streets glisten in the faint, early light. The neighborhood was silent, the houses still and quiet, save for the glowing Christmas decorations dotting the lawns, the ones left on through the night, twinkling reindeer, inflatable Santas, and strings of lights blinking.

But the festive decorations only added to the strange feeling of fear gripping Angie's heart. She ran out into the street, her breath coming in sharp gasps as her eyes scanned the empty road ahead of her.

"Simon!" she shouted, her voice echoing through the stillness. She raced down the block toward the stop sign at the corner, her feet slapping against the wet pavement, her mind racing with worst-case scenarios.

Where is he? How did he make it out of the house? The thought pounded in her head with every step she took, the fear swelling in her chest.

She reached the corner, her breath ragged as she came to a stop. She looked up and down the street, her eyes wide with panic, but there was no sign of Simon. The streets were deserted, the drizzle rain falling in a curtain that obscured her view.

"Come on, come on," she muttered to herself, running a hand through her damp hair. "Where are you?"

Elsewhere in the neighborhood, Simon wandered aimlessly, his feet dragging along the pavement as he stumbled forward. His body moving in slow, disjointed motions, like a puppet with its strings cut. The rain clung to his skin, soaking through his clothes, but he barely felt it. He barely felt anything.

The world around him was a blur of lights and shadows, the Christmas decorations blending together in a strange, dreamlike haze. He staggered off the curb, his body swaying as he walked down the middle of the street, oblivious to his surroundings.

His mind was foggy, the effects of the pills clouding his thoughts, making everything feel distant and unreal. He didn't know where he was going. He just knew he had to keep moving. Keep walking. Keep going.

Back near the Wagner house, Angie ran back up the street to the house, her feet burning from the cold, her heart pounding in her chest. The rain clung to her skin, soaking through her clothes, but she barely noticed. All she could think about was Simon, out there somewhere, lost and alone.

Please, no. Not like this.

She reached her car, fumbling with the keys as her hands trembled. Her mind raced with terrible images of Simon lying unconscious in the gutter, or worse. She couldn't lose him. Not like this.

"No, no, no," she whispered to herself, her voice trembling. "Oh Jesus, not in the gutter. Please."

FOURTEEN

PERFECTLY IMPERFECT

As the early morning light was just creeping over the horizon, Angie found herself driving ever so slowly, afraid to mistake Simon for a deflated Santa. She searched through the neighborhood, her mind traveling back to the days back to when things felt new and uncertain, but exciting.

The cool night air filled Simon's truck as they sat in the driveway outside her house. Angie could still feel the warmth of the evening on her skin, the buzz of excitement from the night out with Simon and his friends. But now, as the evening wound down, the silence between them felt heavier.

Simon turned to her, a small smile tugging at the corner of his mouth. "I hope you had fun."

Angie nodded, her own smile pulling at her lips. "Yeah, yeah it was. Your friends are... a bit crazier than mine."

Simon chuckled, shaking his head. "They ain't no Catholic school girls, that's for sure."

Angie laughed, feeling the tension of the day ease slightly. "No, we're a different kind of crazy. There was that one night we jumped into the ocean topless. That was a wild one."

Simon's eyes widened, his smile turning into a grin. "Whaaat? Sorry I missed that."

Angie laughed, leaning back in her seat, a playful glint in her eyes. "Yep. Lots of hard nips that night."

She could feel Simon's eyes on her as she opened the passenger door and stepped out into the cool evening. Her heart raced a little, not from the conversation, but from the way Simon looked at her, like there was something about her he couldn't get enough of. She liked it, even if it made her a little nervous.

As she turned to head toward the house, Simon called her back, pulling something from the back seat. "Hey, wait a second," he said, motioning her over to the tailgate of his truck. Simon sat down and patted the spot next to him, and she climbed up, their feet dangling off the edge, the cool metal cold beneath her.

He held a small, wrapped box in his hand, his expression suddenly more serious.

"Happy birthday, Angelina," he said, holding out the box toward her.

Angie blinked, surprised. Her birthday. She had nearly forgotten, but Simon hadn't. The gesture made her heart swell, and she took the box from him, her fingers trembling slightly.

"Oh, thank you, Simon," she said, unwrapping the gift with care. Inside was a small, hand-crafted flower vase, delicate and simple, but beautiful in its own way.

For a moment, she stared at it. Before she could stop herself, tears welled up in her eyes. She bowed her head, trying to keep herself together, but the tears spilled over, hot and sudden. She didn't even know why she was crying.

Simon shifted awkwardly, unsure of what to do. He reached out to pat her back but hesitated, pulling his hand back. "Uh, I'm sorry it's simple," he said, his voice uncertain. "I thought it was too soon for jewelry..."

Angie shook her head, her tears falling faster now. "No, it's..." she paused. "It's sweet, thank you, it's lovely. I don't know why I'm crying. I had fun tonight."

"Okay," Simon, his brow furrowing with concern. He didn't push her, didn't ask for more. But Angie could feel the warmth of his presence, the way he was waiting for her to say something more if she wanted to.

Angie gave him a small, tearful smile, "Thank you, Simon."

She thought she could just call it a night and walk away, put the moment behind her. But then Simon's voice, gentle but firm. "Angie. You can tell me if something's wrong."

Something in his tone told her he wasn't going to let her brush this off. She looked at him, meeting his gaze, and for a moment, she felt like she could let go of the wall she was holding up.

"This is gonna seem silly," Angie began, her voice quiet as she looked down at her hands. "But... my dad forgot my birthday." She laughed bitterly, shaking her head. "I keep telling myself it's no big deal, but if it wasn't, then why am I crying?"

Simon didn't say anything right away. He just nodded, letting her words sink in. "That sucks," he said simply, his voice low and calm.

Angie's chest tightened again. "It's not even the first time," she laughed. "I feel like I'm back to being a sad little seven-year-old. My parents had just split up, and I just... I just want my home back, you know? I miss that home feeling."

Simon's brow furrowed, and he looked at her with a seriousness that made her heart ache. "So, he needs to let you know that you're special and not all screwed up."

"Yeah," Angie nodded, her throat tight. "I guess."

They sat in silence for a moment. The sounds of the neighborhood faded into the background, and all Angie could feel was the quiet between them.

Simon broke the silence, his voice softer now. "Would you feel better knowing I'm my parents' disappointment?"

Angie looked at him, surprised by the vulnerability in his voice. He gave a small, rueful smile. "Probably for a few reasons, but the big one is for turning down a swimming scholarship. A good one."

Angie blinked, taken aback. "You did?"

Simon shrugged. "School's not my thing. I didn't want to take someone's money and not want to be there. Whatever. They got my brother to make 'em proud."

"Why is he so special?" Angie asked, curiosity tugging at her.

Simon let out a breath, shaking his head. "Oh, you know. College, good grades, attainable life goals. Boring and sensible."

Angie chuckled. "You're right, pretty high standards. Damn siblings. So what, have they disowned you? Written you out of the will?"

Simon smiled faintly, but there was sadness in his eyes. "No, not that harsh. Just hound me about what I should be doing with my life. Wasted potential, no direction. Constantly comparing me to him. Basic stuff."

Angie looked at him. "So, are you wasting potential?"

Simon shrugged again, his eyes distant. "I don't know. Maybe. I was really good at swimming. My parents were right. I passed up on a good thing."

Angie tilted her head, studying him. "So, you're like this lost little puppy?"

Simon laughed, but there was an edge to it. "Uh-oh, you seeing me like a project? You need to fix me up now?"

Angie shook her head quickly. "No, no. You work on you, and I'll work on me." She hesitated, then added, "Was it too soon to share daddy issues? I feel like it's too soon. You scared off now?"

Simon smirked, leaning back. "I'ma start running."

"Damn," Angie said, playfully smacking his arm. "I knew it. I shoulda waited till like six months in, right? Shit."

"Nah, it's cool," Simon said, his smile widening. "You gotta get to know the crazy sometime."

Angie smiled, feeling the warmth of his words settle over her. "I like talking with you, Simon. It feels weird, but in a good way."

Simon's hand resting gently on hers. "Yeah, I'm picking up what you're layin' down, sugar."

"Are you? You catching the raindrops I'm dropping?" she teased, raising an eyebrow.

Simon laughed, shaking his head. "That's not, no."

Angie grinned. "I liked it."

Simon leaned closer, his voice low. "You soaking up the rays of my sunshine?"

Angie blushed, her heart racing. "Oh, yeah. That's much better."

And before she could say anything more, Simon leaned in and kissed her, the warmth of his lips sending a shiver down her spine. At that moment, everything felt right, like maybe she had found something that could lead her home again.

Back in the present, Angie blinked away the memory, she was lonely but her heart full. Those early days had been so simple, so full of possibility. Now, everything felt heavier.

But she held onto those moments, the small pieces of their beginning, like they could somehow guide her through the chaos they were living in now.

Fifteen

Stranger No Danger

Meanwhile a few blocks away, a kind-faced woman named Norma stood by her bedroom window, peering out into the gloomy morning. She had been getting ready for the day, her house quiet and still, when she noticed a figure wandering aimlessly down the street.

Her brow furrowed as she watched the man, his slow, shuffling movements unsettling in the quiet morning. He looked lost, his eyes blank as he moved down the middle of the road, the rain clinging to him like a second skin.

Norma's heart ached as she watched him, a sense of deep concern settling over her. She didn't recognize him, but something told her he wasn't supposed to be out here. Something wasn't right.

Her husband, Stan, was seated at the kitchen table, reading the newspaper, blissfully unaware of what was happening outside. Norma's voice trembled slightly as she broke the silence.

"Honey, there's a young man outside," she said, her eyes still fixed on the window. "Uh, he... well, he doesn't look good."

Stan didn't look up from his paper. "What do you mean?"

Norma turned to face him, her worry etched in every line of her face. "Go look, you'll see."

Stan finally glanced up, raising an eyebrow. "Is he gonna kill me? You want me dead, woman?"

"Oh stop," Norma scolded, shaking her head. "He doesn't look mean, just... not right."

Stan sighed, folding his paper as he stood. "Alright, alright. I'll go see what's going on."

Stan stepped out of the house, Norma right behind him. He squinted as he spotted Simon, his brow furrowing in confusion.

"What the hell?" Stan muttered, then called out. "Hey buddy, you alright?"

Simon turned slowly, his eyes glazed and unfocused. "Sir am," he slurred, barely able to keep his balance.

Stan took a cautious step forward. "I'm just wondering why you're walking in the middle of the street? You have to watch out for cars, you know."

"Oh, okay," Simon mumbled. "I'm sorry."

His body swayed again, and he stumbled toward the curb. Instinctively, Stan reached out, taking Simon's arm to steady him. He guided him to the curb, gently lowering him to sit down.

Norma hovered nearby, her worry deepening. "Are you hurt at all? You alright?" she asked.

Simon shivered slightly, his body trembling in the cool morning air. "I'm cold," he muttered, his voice barely above a whisper.

Stan glanced at Norma, his eyes narrowing. "Look at him. He's not drunk. He doesn't smell like alcohol. Is he high? If the cops see him like this, they'll pick him up for sure."

Norma's heart ached as she looked at Simon, who sat slumped on the curb like a lost child. She reached out, her voice soothing. "You go ahead and sit right here, dear. I'll get you a blanket."

Turning to Stan, she added quietly, "We'll wait with him a bit. Maybe he'll sober up." She paused, then offered a smile. "Coffee?"

Stan nodded, keeping a watchful eye on Simon. "How about some coffee? We just made some," he said.

Norma hurried back inside, returning moments later with a warm blanket and a steaming cup of coffee. She handed the blanket to Stan, who draped it over Simon's shoulders as he shivered.

Simon barely reacted, his body hunched against the cold. "That's good," he muttered, his words slurred.

Angie drove slowly through the empty streets, her eyes scanning the neighborhood desperately. Her hands gripped the steering wheel tightly, her knuckles white with tension. She had been driving in circles for what felt like hours, but there was no sign of Simon.

She pulled the car to a stop in the middle of the street, her head resting on the steering wheel. Her chest felt tight, the fear gnawing at her insides. She looked up, her eyes brimming with tears as she whispered a plea to the heavens.

"Please Lord," she murmured, her voice cracking. "Please let me find him."

With a deep breath, she turned the corner, and as the car rolled slowly down the block, her heart leapt into her throat. There, half a block ahead, she saw him seated on the curb with two strangers.

Angie let out a shaky sigh of relief, her whole body trembling as she pulled the car over to the side of the road. She quickly made a three-point turn to park the car, her heart still racing as she stepped out.

Stan and Norma watched as Angie approached, her face pale with worry. The early morning mist, which clung to her hair and clothes, started to lift. Her hands shook slightly as she walked up to them, as if the fading chill couldn't quite take her unease with it.

Stan raised an eyebrow, his voice gentle but firm. "You know him? Does he belong to you?"

Angie nodded, her throat tight. "Yes," she said. "He's my husband."

Norma gave Angie a small, understanding smile. "We saw him wandering in the street," she explained. "He could barely walk. We didn't want him to get hurt."

Angie's chest tightened as she looked at Simon, who sat slumped on the curb, his body trembling under the blanket. "Thank you," she whispered, her voice barely audible. "I'm sorry we bothered you."

"No bother, honey," Stan said, standing and offering his hand to Simon. "Okay son, let's get you in the car."

Simon struggled to stand, his movements slow and unsteady. Stan helped him to his feet, guiding him toward the car as Simon shuffled like a man far older than his years, his body shaking, his eyes glazed over.

"You gotta get off of that stuff, son. You got a nice wife here, you know," Stan said to Simon with fatherly concern as he helped him buckle up.

Angie bit her lip, fighting back the tears that threatened to spill over. She wanted to be strong, but seeing Simon like this, so lost, so out of it, broke her heart all over again.

Norma stepped forward, wrapping Angie in a warm hug. Angie hesitated for a moment, then melted into the embrace, the tears she had been holding back finally spilling over.

"Hang in there, dear," Norma whispered, her voice full of quiet strength.

Angie nodded, "Thank you," she whispered, wiping her eyes. Her heart aching as she got in the car and pulled away.

SIXTEEN

IS THIS CRAZY YET?

A few moments later, Angie pulled up in front of their house. She helped Simon out of the car, his movements slow and disjointed. She took a deep breath.

He stood by the car, his hand gripping the door frame for support. His body swayed slightly, one foot dragging against the ground as if it was anchored in, too much to lift. He dusted his other foot on the ground like a tired old horse, and as he stepped away from the car, he lost his balance.

They both tumbled onto the front lawn, Simon sprawled out like a snow angel, his body limp. Angie lay caught beneath his arm, her face pressed into the grass, her butt awkwardly raised in the air. She let out a long sigh, her body too tired to fight anymore.

She tried to roll him over, but Simon was dead weight, his body unresponsive. Her feet slipped in the wet grass, and after a few more failed attempts, she gave up.

"Wait here," she muttered, her voice tired and defeated.

Angie's breath was ragged as she bolted into the house, her heart pounding in her chest. The early morning light was creeping through the windows, but all she could focus on was Simon, still sprawled on the grass outside. She sprinted up the stairs, taking them two at a time, her feet barely making a sound on the carpeted steps.

Reaching her in-laws' bedroom door, she pressed her ear against it, her heart racing. The sound of the shower running echoed faintly through the door, but she needed help now. Without thinking, she knocked, her knuckles gently tapping at first.

"Dad?" she called out, her voice barely above a whisper. When there was no response, she knocked louder, her voice trembling. "Dad?"

Still nothing.

Her panic surged, and she pushed the door open a crack. Hank, Simon's father, lay fast asleep in bed, oblivious to the commotion outside. Angie's pulse quickened as she stepped fully into the room.

"Hank?" she said, louder now, her voice tight with urgency.

Hank stirred, blinking groggily, his face still lost in sleep. "Huh? Yeah?"

"I'm sorry," Angie said, her voice catching in her throat, "but I need your help. It's Simon. I can't move him. He's on the grass..."

The words seemed to snap Hank into focus. His face hardened with concern as he fumbled out of bed, his body sluggish with sleep as he grabbed for his pants. Angie turned and bolted back down the stairs, the adrenaline driving her forward. She needed to get back to Simon.

Outside, Simon was barely conscious, his body twisted awkwardly on the lawn like a child struggling to roll over. His shirt had ridden up, revealing a patch on his lower back. The sight of it sent a jolt through Angie. Her eyes locked on the small square of adhesive, and without thinking, she ripped it off, shoving it into her pocket as Hank stepped out of the house.

Hank froze for a moment, the sight of his son slumped on the ground cutting through him like a knife. His face tightened, years of worry and disappointment settling over him as he made his way toward Simon. Angie knelt beside Simon, her breath coming in short gasps as she tried to steady him, but he was too heavy, too far gone to help himself.

Together, Hank and Angie lifted Simon, their muscles trembling as they struggled to get him upright. Simon's legs barely cooperating as they dragged him toward the house. His head lolled to the side, his eyes half-closed, glazed over with a distant, foggy look.

The family cat watched from its perch on the porch railing, its eyes wide and curious, oblivious to the chaos unfolding below.

Inside, the living room was dimly lit, the curtains still drawn as Hank and Angie maneuvered Simon onto the couch. He slumped into the cushions, his body limp and unresponsive. The once-warm, familiar space now felt suffocating to Angie, every breath she took weighed down by the tension filling the room.

Hank stood over Simon, his hands resting on his hips as he looked down at his son, his face etched with a mixture of anger and helplessness. "What the hell happened?" he asked, his voice low but sharp.

Angie stood beside him, her hands trembling as she wiped them on her pants. "I don't know," she admitted, her voice shaky. "He took too many pills. Went for a walk... I had to find him."

Hank let out a long breath, shaking his head as he stared at Simon's unconscious form. "This can't keep happening," he muttered, his voice thick with frustration. "What is he doing to himself?" He paused, glancing at Angie. "I'm sorry you have to see this too."

Angie's chest tightened, her heart aching as she looked at Simon, the man she loved but barely recognized at this moment. "I just want to help him," she whispered, her voice small.

Hank sighed with resignation. "Yeah, I know," he said quietly. "I think we're past that."

Before either of them could say more, the sound of hurried footsteps echoed down the stairs. Susan, Simon's mother, rushed into the room, her face pale with worry as she took in the scene before her.

"What's going on?" she asked, her voice tinged with panic. "What happened? Is he okay?"

She hurried to Simon's side, her hands reaching out to touch his face, her fingers trembling as she smoothed his hair back. Angie felt herself being pushed aside, the familiar sting of being replaced by a mother's fierce protectiveness.

"He took too many pills," Hank explained, his voice flat. "Angie brought him home."

Susan's eyes darted to Angie, her expression a mixture of shock and confusion. "What? Brought him home? From where?"

Angie, her throat tight with emotion. "I don't know," she admitted, her voice barely above a whisper. "I woke up, and he was gone."

Susan's face tightened, the frustration spilling over. "Why didn't you wake me up? I could have stopped him."

"I'm sorry," Angie said, her voice trembling. "I didn't think about that when I was half asleep."

Susan shook her head, her attention snapping back to Simon. "Is he okay here?" she asked, her voice rising with anxiety. "Shouldn't we get him upstairs? We should call an ambulance. This couch isn't comfortable for him. Shouldn't we keep him awake?"

Hank's voice cut through the panic, firm and steady. "No, no," he said. "He's too out of it right now. Just leave him there. Let him sleep it off for a few hours." Without waiting for a response, Hank turned and headed back up the stairs.

Susan watched him go, her frustration bubbling just beneath the surface. "Wait, Hank," she called after him. "We need to talk about this."

Hank paused at the bottom of the stairs, his voice weary. "Yes, we do," he said, his tone clipped. "We'll talk about this *again* but not now."

Susan's face flushed with anger, her voice rising. "Hank!"

"Don't start, Susan," Hank said, his voice firm. "There's no sense in talking now. He's out. We're the ones getting worked up. Just leave it for later."

Susan's shoulders sagged as Hank disappeared up the stairs. She knelt beside Simon, her hand resting gently on his forehead, her fingers brushing through his hair. He looked so fragile, so far from the strong, capable son she had raised. Her heart ached as she whispered, almost to herself, "This is why I need to know what happens in this house."

Angie stood nearby, her body tense, her hands clenched into fists at her sides. She felt like an outsider in her own life, caught in a battle between a mother's protectiveness and a wife's helplessness.

Hank's voice floated down from the stairs, his words sharp but tired. "Leave the poor girl alone, Susan. She's not doing this to him."

Angie with a lump in her throat, her voice barely audible as she whispered, "I'm sorry."

Seventeen

Coffee, Chaos, Repeat

Angie had always prided herself on being able to handle things. Work. Life. Simon. It had become a delicate balancing act, and though she wouldn't admit it to anyone, not even herself, she could feel it all slipping.

The warehouse was lined with tall metal shelves and stacked deep with boxes. Metal fasteners, nuts and bolts, all shapes and sizes each one tagged with its aircraft part number, each one vital to something that would eventually soar through the sky. But down here, it was all just inventory. Labeled boxes, coded with methodical precision. Dusty, and seemingly endless.

Angie made her way to the second level of the warehouse, up the grated metal steps. The warehouse felt both cavernous and stifling, the kind of place that boxed you in with its monotony. She balanced a coffee in one hand and a box of fasteners in the other but her mind was somewhere far away.

"Benny, we got the 3A Fasteners in!" she shouted, trying to focus on the task at hand.

From somewhere in the racks of shelves, Benjamin called out, "I'll be right there!"

Angie nodded to herself. *Just keep going.* As she took the next step, the bottom of the box in her hands gave way, and as she tried to catch it, she fell forward with her coffee breaking her fall, hot liquid spilling down her shirt. She tumbled forward and hit the steel steps with a thud, the sound of 5,000 tiny fasteners spilling out in a cacophony of metal clinking against metal.

She lay still for a moment, her head resting on the steel step, her eyes closing as she took the unwanted rest. The pain from the hot coffee, the embarrassment, she let it wash over her.

The world around her blurred, and all she could hear was the sound of her own breathing. Her mind slipped, taking her somewhere else. Somewhere she hadn't been in a long time.

Eighteen

Not the Ugly Cry

The music pulsed through the walls of the house, the bass reverberating through Angie's chest as she stood in front of the mirror in the crowded bathroom. She wiped her lips, making them glossy, her fingers trembling slightly as she adjusted her top. It was New Year's Eve, just minutes before midnight, but she didn't feel the excitement she should have felt.

Angie glanced at her own reflection again, forcing a smile that didn't quite reach her eyes. She took a sip of her drink, the alcohol burning its way down her throat.

Her mind was buzzing with thoughts of Simon and even though they weren't officially a couple, she scoured the house for him. Angie couldn't help but feel a growing sense of dread in her stomach.

As the countdown to midnight began, her heart was pounding in time with the music. The house was packed with people, all laughing, drinking, and celebrating. Angie moved through the crowd, her eyes scanning the faces, looking for Simon.

"Five, four, three, two... Happy New Year!" The cheers erupted around her as the clock struck midnight, but Angie barely registered it. Her heart stopped as she spotted Simon across the backyard, a beer in hand, his lips locked with another girl, dirty blond hair, too much eyeliner, and a cut-off Roxy tank top that left nothing to the imagination.

Angie's chest tightened, her breath catching in her throat as her eyes filled with tears. Before she could even process what was happening, she watched in horror as another girl, this one dressed just as trashy, pulled Simon's arm, and he kissed her, too.

It felt like the ground had been ripped out from under her. She was frozen, standing there while everyone around her celebrated the new year. Tears blurred her vision as Simon took another swig of his beer and finally noticed her standing near the sliding door.

Angie's stomach churned, her heart pounding in her chest as she turned and fled the house, tears spilling down her cheeks. The cool night air hit her like a slap to the face, but it did nothing to soothe the ache in her chest.

"Angie! Hey, Ang!" Simon's voice called out from behind her, but she kept walking, the tears blurring her vision as she wiped them away with the back of her hand.

She stopped at the end of the driveway, her chest heaving as she tried to catch her breath. Simon caught up to her, his steps unsteady, the beer still sloshing in his hand.

"You know we're not locked down, right?" he said, his voice casual, as if the sight of him with those girls hadn't just shattered her heart.

Angie's chest tightened, and she turned to face him, her eyes filled with confusion and hurt. "Then what am I doing here?"

"I didn't invite you," Simon replied, his voice blunt.

Angie's lip quivered, and she wiped angrily at her tears. "I'm so fucking confused, Simon," she said, her voice breaking. "I don't get this. And now I'm one of those girls that ugly cries when she's drunk, and I *hate* those kinds of girls!"

"Dude, we've just been hanging out. Casual. I told you, I don't call chicks girlfriend for a reason," Simon said with a shrug, like it was the simplest thing in the world.

Angie stared at him, his words cracking her heart like ice. "Ok, dude. I see. I'm crazy," she said, her voice trembling. "Not only are you my first *everything*, but stupid me thought there was a connection thing, I guess that's all in my head... AND you gave me a necklace."

Simon sighed, running a hand through his hair. "I told you," he said quietly. "You need to experience more than me. Please."

Angie's heart clenched. "Why? Why can't I know that you're it for me?"

"It don't work like that, sugar. You gotta go be free and sow some wild oats," Simon replied, his voice softer now, as if trying to be kind.

"There are no oats to sow," Angie snapped, her anger flaring. "It's just a small patch that needs an occasional plow!"

Simon shook his head, laughing and smiling sadly. "What happens in fifteen years when we're old and you start to wonder, could I have done better?"

Angie blinked, her eyes wide with disbelief. "No," she said, shaking her head.

At the same time, Simon answers, "Yes."

"You're gonna regret me, Ang," Simon said, his voice steady.

Tears streamed down Angie's face as she stood there, the pain of his words cutting deep. "You got me outta my shell," she said, her voice cracking. "Made me feel good about being me. I see you too. You're scared cause of a past heartache. But go ahead, have fun with your trashy hoes. That'll fix it. Don't forget to double wrap your shit."

With a quick yank, Angie broke the small ruby necklace from her neck and dropped it at Simon's feet before turning and walking away.

Simon sighed heavily and headed back toward the house.

Angie couldn't resist. She ran back, picked up the necklace, and stuffed it into her pocket.

Around the corner, Angie sank down against a brick wall, her knees pulled to her chest as the tears came in full force.

NINETEEN

B-A-N-A-N-A-S

The cold steel of the steps pressed against Angie's cheek as her eyes fluttered open. The memory of that New Year's Eve faded, leaving behind a hollow ache in her chest.

"Angie!" Benjamin's voice cut through the fog as he ran out from between the shelves, his footsteps echoing in the large space. "You alright?"

A few other workers appeared, including Erica, who stood at the bottom of the steps with a concerned look on her face.

Carl, one of the warehouse guys, couldn't resist a joke. "You dropped something, boss."

Angie's frustration boiled over. "Did I, Carl? Did I just spill hot coffee on my tits and fall flat on my face? Did that just happen?"

Carl held his hands up, shrugging. "It was just an observation."

"Well, thank you for sharing, captain obvious," Angie snapped.

Erica, always the peacemaker, stepped in. "Shut up, Carl," she said, then turned to Angie with a sympathetic smile. "Let's get you cleaned up."

"It's fine. I'm fine. Everything is fine," Angie muttered, brushing off Erica's concern. But as she looked at the mess of fasteners scattered across the floor, her frustration turned into a bitter laugh. "The poor little fasteners. They're all lost now."

Erica placed a gentle hand on Angie's shoulder. "It's okay. We've got magnets. Carl will clean it up."

Carl groaned. "But why me? I was just being funny."

"Shut it, Carl," Benjamin barked, guiding Carl toward the spilled fasteners. "Come on."

Erica's arm wrapped firmly around Angie's shoulders as they walked away from the scattered fasteners and spilled coffee. The cold warehouse air contrasted sharply with the burning frustration bubbling under Angie's skin. Her body felt tense, her mind racing, but there was a hollow ache sitting deep inside her, one that no amount of work or routine could distract her from.

"You need to go home," Erica said, her voice steady but filled with concern. "It's been a full day for you already."

Angie managed a dry laugh, her throat tight. "I'm literally a hot mess. Ugh, my boobs... my boobs hurt so much right now."

Erica squeezed her shoulder gently, trying to lighten the mood. "Well, good thing they're petite."

Angie gave a weak smile, but it didn't reach her eyes. The pain in her chest wasn't just from the coffee. "Are you okay?" Erica asked, her tone shifting from playful to serious.

Angie's heart clenched as she shook her head, her voice small. "No."

Erica sighed, glancing over at her with sympathy. "I won't tell if you want to run away."

Angie let out a bitter chuckle, but it quickly dissolved into something more vulnerable. "Nobody asks to be sick like this, you know? Nobody asks to love someone who's sick like this." Her words unsteady as they sank in. "I don't blame anyone if they have to leave. I just... I just know I can't."

There it was. The truth she had been carrying with her, the burden that had grown heavier each day. She couldn't leave Simon, even if everything inside her screamed that she should.

Erica stopped walking and turned to face her. "You're a strong woman there, Mrs. Wagner. Don't forget that."

The words "strong woman" echoed in Angie's mind, but they didn't feel like enough. Not today. Not after everything.

Minutes later, Angie sat behind the wheel of her car, her coffee-stained shirt sticking to her skin. The cool air from the car's vents did nothing to ease the burning frustration and the mess of emotions swirling inside her. She stared out at the stretch of road lined with orchards, the trees a blur as she pressed the gas pedal harder, wanting to outrun the morning's events.

Her fingers fumbled over the radio preset buttons, seeking distraction, anything to fill the silence in the car. Finally, Gwen Stefani's "Hollaback Girl" blasted through the speakers, the beat loud and unapologetic.

Angie turned the volume up, way up. The music pounded through the car, shaking the windows, and Angie felt the rhythm wash over her. For a moment, she let the beat carry her away, singing along loudly, her voice cracking as she yelled out the lyrics, trying to drown out her thoughts.

"This shit is bananas, B-A-N-A-N-A-S!" she belted, her voice off-key but filled with raw emotion.

And then it hit her.

The tears came suddenly, uncontrollably, spilling down her cheeks as she sang. The absurdity of it all. The chaos, the frustration, the broken promises pushed her over the edge.

Angie flipped a U-turn in the middle of the road, not caring if anyone saw her, and drove back down the stretch again, just to feel like she had control of something. But even as the car sped forward, she couldn't escape the tears that blurred her vision.

TWENTY

CHERRY ON TOP

When Angie pulled up in front of the house, her body felt exhausted. Her red, swollen eyes stung from crying, and the coffee-stained shirt was uncomfortable against her skin. As she dragged herself through the front door, she dropped her purse and lunch bag onto the floor, her ragdoll accessories trailing behind her.

The house was eerily quiet, the only sound coming from the faint trickle of running water from the downstairs bathroom. Angie let out a long sigh, her body collapsing onto the floor next to the empty couch. She leaned her head back against the cushions, her eyes fluttering shut as she tried to steady her breathing.

But the quiet only made the silence in her head louder. Everything felt like it was slipping away including her sense of control, her patience, her hope.

In the bathroom, Simon splashed water onto his face, his reflection in the mirror blurred and distorted. His head throbbed, but the cold water helped clear his mind at least a little. He stared at himself, his eyes bloodshot, his skin pale.

He barely recognized the man in the mirror anymore.

After a moment, Simon wiped his face with a towel and exited the bathroom, his movements slow and deliberate. As he stepped into the living room, his eyes landed on Angie, sitting on the floor by the couch, her face a mixture of exhaustion and defeat.

"What happened to you?" Simon asked, his voice still groggy.

Angie didn't look up at him, her fingers tracing the fabric of the couch as she spoke, her voice flat. "It's time for me to move out. I don't even know where to start with what happened this morning."

Simon blinked, his stomach twisting. "Can I come with you?"

Angie let out a bitter laugh, shaking her head. "I can probably find a crappy little studio. I can use the front door money for a deposit."

Simon managed a small smile, but it didn't reach his eyes. "That might be nice. You smell like coffee."

"Yeah, I topped off the morning by testing my tit durability," Angie muttered, the sarcasm in her voice barely hiding the pain beneath it.

Simon's face showed the guilt creeping in. "I'm sorry about this morning," he said quietly.

Angie looked up at him then, her eyes red and tired. "Do you even remember it?"

Simon hesitated, his gaze dropping to the floor. "A glimpse or two."

Angie reached into her pocket and pulled out the patch she had ripped from his back earlier, holding it out to him with a weary expression. "Here," she said, her voice barely a whisper. "I don't know what that shit is, but it's gonna kill you."

Simon took the patch from her, his fingers brushing against hers for the briefest moment before he looked away, ashamed.

Angie stood up, gathering her things with slow, deliberate movements. The silence in the room was almost unbearable, each second stretching on as they stood there, both knowing that something had shifted between them.

Simon reached for her hand, his touch gentle and hesitant. "I'm sorry, Angelina," he whispered, his voice filled with regret. "I didn't mean to drag you into all this."

Angie closed her eyes, her chest tightening. She wanted to tell him it was okay, that she understood, but the words wouldn't come. She knew the truth, this wasn't something she could fix.

"I know," she said softly, her voice thick with emotion.

Simon looked at her, his eyes pleading. "Can I come with you?"

Angie stared at him, her heart breaking as she realized she didn't have an answer. She couldn't give him what he wanted.

Without a word, she turned and walked toward the door, leaving Simon standing there.

Later that evening...

As the hallway was dimly lit, the muted glow from the night-light cast long shadows along the walls. Simon stood outside his parents' bedroom door, his ear pressed to the wood as their voices filtered through. He didn't mean to eavesdrop, but the tone of their argument had drawn him in. It was quiet, strained, filled with years of frustration and disappointment.

"Bullshit, Susan. The drugs are why his brother doesn't talk to him," Hank's voice was rough, edged with anger and exhaustion.

Susan's response came quickly, sharp and defensive. "It's not his fault. He'd be fine if he hadn't wrecked that bike, he'd be fine."

Simon winced, the words sinking deep. The accident. It always came back to the accident. His heart pounded in his chest, the familiar knot of guilt tightening in his stomach. He pressed his hand against the door as if the pressure might somehow block out the sound.

"You can't keep doing this," Hank continued, his voice breaking slightly. "It's time for us to cut him loose. We've said this too many times now. We keep bending, and nothing changes."

Simon felt his breath hitch, his chest tightening as his father's words hit him like a punch to the gut. His throat burned, and he fought the urge to push the door open right then, to defend himself, to explain. But the truth was, he had no defense. He knew Hank was right.

"But he's married now," Susan's voice searching for hope. "What about her?"

"That's for him to screw up. We're done. It's time, okay? We need to be done with the stress of it all. We have to let him go," Hank's voice was resolute, final.

Simon had heard enough. His heart pounded in his chest, each word from his father echoing in his mind. He raised his fist and knocked, the sound loud and awkward in the stillness of the hallway. Without waiting for a response, he opened the door.

His parents turned to face him, their expressions a mixture of surprise and discomfort. Susan's face was flushed, her eyes wide with concern, while Hank looked worn down.

"Mom, Dad..." Simon began, his voice rough, barely able to find the words. "I just wanted to say sorry." He cleared his throat, his gaze dropping to the floor as he struggled to get the words out. "I know I've been a burden, and I know it's not easy on you."

Susan's eyes softened, her hand rising to her mouth as if to stop herself from speaking, but Hank remained silent, his face unreadable.

"Um, so... Angie and I are moving out," Simon continued, his voice trembling slightly. "I think it's time, and I just wanted you to know."

Hank's expression didn't change, but there was a flicker of something. Maybe relief crossed his features. "That's good news, son," he said quietly. "That's good."

Simon nodded, his throat tight, waiting for something, anything that felt like approval or understanding. But what came next shattered what little hope he had left.

"You know what?" Hank's voice was steady, but the words cut deep. "Once you move out, it's probably best we don't have daily contact with you for a little while. I hope you understand... we need a little space, that's all. All this has been hard."

He couldn't bring himself to look his father in the eyes. His chest tightened, and he felt his breath catch in his throat.

"Alright, Pop," Simon whispered, his voice breaking. "I get it. You finally get your empty nest, right?" He forced a smile, but it didn't reach his eyes. "Okay. Goodnight."

Before they could respond, Simon turned and shut the door behind him, the sound of it closing reverberating in the quiet hallway.

Simon made his way down the stairs, each step feeling heavier than the last. His mind was spinning, his emotions tangled in a mess of guilt, shame, and anger. The words from his father's mouth played on repeat in his head, drowning out everything else.

"It's done," Hank's voice echoed behind the closed door. "He knows, and we do need time for us, or else we'll fall apart again."

Simon's hand tightened around the banister as he descended the final step. *Fall apart again.* That's what he was doing to them. To all of them.

In the kitchen, the hum of the refrigerator was the only sound. The cool air hit Simon's face as he opened the door, his eyes scanning the shelves, looking for something to distract him from the emptiness gnawing at his insides.

His gaze landed on the can of whipped cream, tucked behind a carton of eggs. He grabbed it, shaking the can with a trembling hand as his emotions bubbled dangerously close to the surface. Tears stung his eyes, and he cursed under his breath, trying to hold it all back.

But when he pressed the nozzle and filled his mouth with the sweetness, it was as if something broke inside him. The tears that had been threatening all night finally spilled over, hot and unrelenting. He let them fall, his back leaning against the counter as he sank to the floor, the whipped cream can clutched in his hand like a lifeline.

His shoulders shook with silent sobs, the tears mixing with the lingering sweetness of the whipped cream. For a moment, everything felt surreal. Like he was watching his life unfold from a distance, powerless to stop the wreckage.

Twenty-One

Don't Forget to Breathe

The front door creaked open, revealing a small, cozy studio apartment with just enough charm to make it feel like a fresh start. The apartment was modest, barely a step up from the room with her In-Laws, but it had a quaint porch that overlooked the street below. To Angie, it felt like a tiny refuge from the chaos of her life.

Angie followed the apartment manager inside as she gave a quick tour, her words barely registering. It didn't take long. The entire tour lasted no more than five seconds before the manager turned to Angie with a practiced smile, handing her the keys in exchange for the deposit check. Angie's fingers trembled slightly as she passed over the payment, the metal of the keys cold in her hand.

"Welcome home," the manager said brightly before stepping out and closing the door behind her.

A few days later, Angie stood in the center of the small space, taking it in. Thrift store furniture filled the room: a faded armchair, a second-hand coffee table, and a futon that creaked when she sat on it. Boxes were scattered everywhere, a few wedding gifts like towels and kitchenware had already been neatly placed in the tiny kitchenette, and framed pictures sat on the floor, waiting for their spot on the wall. A curtain divider had been hung up to create a semblance of a bedroom, offering just a little privacy in the small, open space.

Her mom, Sofia, moved quietly around the apartment, unpacking boxes and trying to make it feel like home. Angie was grateful for her mother's presence and quiet support that didn't ask too many questions.

Before leaving for the evening, Sofia placed a small vase of flowers on the coffee table. "Just a little color," she said softly, kissing Angie on the head. As the door closed behind her, Angie sat on the futon alone in the small space that felt too big.

She flipped on the TV, the familiar ticking of the show *24* filling the silence. Her bowl of ramen noodles sat untouched on her lap, steam rising slowly. She lifted her hand, staring down at the wedding ring on her finger, the metal cool against her skin. Everything felt heavy.

Across town, in a dimly lit house, Simon sat on a worn-out couch, the flickering light of the TV casting shadows across the room. His duffle bag, a jacket, and a blanket were piled haphazardly next to him. He leaned back, exhaustion weighing him down as the familiar chaos of *Cops* blared from the screen.

Freddy and Fish moved around him, the smell of greasy pizza wafting through the air as Freddy dropped a box onto the coffee table. Fish settled beside Simon, a bong in hand, offering it up like an old ritual they had repeated countless times before.

Simon hesitated, his eyes lingering on the bong for a moment before he shook his head. "Nah, I'm good," he mumbled, his voice hoarse.

Fish shrugged and took a hit himself, the smoke swirling in the air around them. Freddy laughed as he grabbed the bong next, the haze of their lives wrapped up in a cycle of temporary highs. Simon stared at them blankly, feeling like he was watching from a distance, like he wasn't really there.

His fingers brushed against the metal of his wedding ring, and he clenched his hand into a fist, the pressure grounding him in the present, but also serving as a reminder of everything in suspension. The noise of the TV, the laughter of his friends, it all felt so far away.

Twenty-Two

Suck It In

The cool morning air brushed against Angie's face as she sat on the edge of the loading dock, her coffee cup warming her hands. The noise of the warehouse was a familiar soundtrack, but today, it felt muted. Her thoughts swirled, scattered and unfocused, drifting back to Simon, to the small studio apartment that now felt too quiet, too still.

She was lost in her thoughts when Benjamin quietly joined her on the dock. He didn't say anything at first, just sat down next to her, his presence calm and steady. Angie appreciated that about Benjamin, he never pried, never pushed.

"You know," he finally said, "I don't need to know all the details to know you're going through something."

Angie sighed, rubbing her fingers over the rim of her coffee cup. "Uh, yeah," she said, her voice thick with unspoken emotion. "I guess I haven't done the best job of keeping it out of here. I'm sorry."

"Don't be," Benjamin replied, his tone gentle. "It's quite normal to have bad days."

"Yeah, I guess," Angie muttered, her eyes fixed on the concrete below. "But it's embarrassing."

Benjamin took a sip of his own coffee, letting her words hang in the air for a moment before he responded. "It's not. Life weathers us all a little differently."

Angie nodded, her throat tightening as she tried to find the words to explain, but nothing felt right. After a long pause, she finally spoke, her voice barely above a whisper. "My husband... he's having issues with pain management."

Benjamin's expression showed concern but he didn't ask for more details. He simply nodded, understanding without judgment. "You know, they have a support group over at St. Francis," he said, carefully pulling a pamphlet from his jacket pocket. "It's for people who know someone with issues. I grew up with a parent who drank, and those meetings helped."

Angie hesitated, glancing down at the pamphlet as Benjamin held it out to her. She wasn't sure she was ready to face a support group, wasn't sure if she was ready to admit how bad things had gotten. "Um, okay," she said, her voice wavering. "I don't know if I need that though."

Benjamin smiled, his voice steady and kind. "Maybe you don't. But it might be worth checking out." He pressed the pamphlet into her hand, giving her a reassuring look. "Tuesday nights at 7."

Angie looked down at the pamphlet in her hands, her reality settling in heavier than before. "Thank you, Benjamin," she whispered, her voice thick with gratitude she wasn't sure how to express.

"Sure, kid," Benjamin said, standing up and giving her a small nod.

"Benny, how'd you know?" She asked, her curiosity evident.

Benjamin replied, "It's that look of worry, it's different from others...and my gut." He paused for a moment, then added,

"Sometimes it's nice to be around people who feel crazy because of someone else's crazy."

Angie let out a quiet laugh, though the sound was tinged with sadness. "Yeah," she said, her fingers tightening around the pamphlet. "I guess it would be."

Twenty-Three

Sweet, Sweet Mess

It had been a few weeks since Angie and Simon had seen each other in person. Their conversations had been brief, scattered phone calls never quite addressing the deep void growing between them. Despite the communication, there was a distance neither of them seemed able to bridge. Until tonight.

The evening light filtered through the small window of the studio apartment, casting long shadows across the thrift store furniture and giving the space an almost fragile warmth. Angie sat on the edge of the futon, her heart pounding in her chest as she glanced around the room, making sure everything was in its place.

The knock on the door startled her out of her thoughts. Angie stood up, smoothing down her shirt before walking to the door, her hand trembling slightly as she reached for the knob. She hesitated for just a second before pulling the door open.

There he was, Simon, standing in the doorway with his bags at his feet. He looked tired, worn down, but there was something else in his eyes, something that mirrored the same uncertainty and longing that Angie had been carrying since they'd been apart.

For a moment, neither of them moved. The air between them crackled with an electricity that neither wanted to acknowledge too quickly. They didn't want to seem too eager, too desperate for the comfort of each other.

"Hi," Angie said softly, stepping aside to let him in. "Come in."

Simon glanced around the small apartment, his eyes briefly landing on the futon, the clutter of boxes, and the dishes in the sink. "This is nice," he said, his voice quiet.

Angie shrugged, folding her arms over her chest. "It's small."

Simon shook his head, giving her a small smile. "No, you did good. It's fine."

"Here," Angie said, gesturing toward the futon. "Put your stuff down. We have a futon now."

Simon nodded, dropping his bags by the futon and looking around the room again. There was something unspoken between. They were together, but it didn't feel the same. Not yet.

"I see," Simon said, glancing at the baking dishes stacked in the sink.

Angie caught the direction of his gaze and let out a quiet laugh. "So... kitchen, bedroom, bathroom," she said, motioning around the small space. "Welcome home, I guess."

Simon met her eyes, his expression uncertain. "I wasn't sure you wanted me here."

Angie's heart ached at his words. "Of course I want you," she said. "And here."

Simon ran a hand through his hair, sighing. "I want you too, so... why does it feel weird to be here?"

Angie walked over to the futon and sat down, swinging her feet slightly as if to ease the tension. "Because we don't know what we're doing," she admitted, her voice barely above a whisper. "Because being apart doesn't feel right. I want us together, but... I don't think you can be on those pills anymore."

The mention of the pills caused Simon's face to harden slightly. "Oh, here we go," he muttered, taking a seat on the edge of the futon, not looking at her. "I've told you, I take the pain pills for the pain. The muscle relaxers help ease the spasms, and the anxiety ones calm my worry about the pain. It's fine. My body is used to it."

Angie sighed, her frustration bubbling up as she stood and walked over to the sink in the *not really a kitchen* space. She grabbed a frying pan and a sponge, scrubbing furiously. "Si, you OD'd. Probably from adding in that plastic patch thingy."

Simon crossed his arms, his jaw tightening. "Not really."

Angie shot him a look over her shoulder, her hands still scrubbing the burnt remnants of dinner off the pan. "Uh, yes," she said, her voice sharper now. "Anytime you lose your shit like that, it's technically a dose over what should be."

Simon didn't argue, but his silence was enough of a confirmation. "I suppose that's correct," he muttered.

Angie turned back to the sink, her movements more forceful as she attacked the next pan. "Look at you now," she said, her voice softening just a bit. "You're sober."

Simon leaned back, rubbing his face with both hands. "No, I'm not," he said, his voice strained. "I'm just running low, and I'm in fuckin' pain."

Angie's heart clenched at his words, but she didn't turn around. She kept scrubbing the pan, her frustration spilling over into her movements. "I don't think you're in pain," she said, the words slipping out before she could stop them.

"I can't sit on my ass without being in pain," Simon shot back, his voice rising with frustration. "I hurt all the time. Standing, kneeling, sleeping."

"Well, you don't look like it," Angie replied, her voice biting.

Simon let out a sharp laugh, shaking his head. "You'd rather I be crippled? In bandages and crutches?"

Angie slammed the pan down into the sink, her hands trembling as she turned to face him. "It would be easier to see that you needed pills, yes," she admitted, her voice thick with emotion.

Simon stood up, the tension between them thickening. "I need pills to help me feel normal," he said, his voice breaking slightly.

Angie shook her head, her eyes brimming with tears. "Your normal is stupid."

"Being in pain is not normal, Angie," Simon snapped, stepping closer to her. "You missed a spot."

Angie looked down at the pan, her anger flaring. "It's burnt cheese. It won't come off. It's a new non-stick pan, and it won't come off."

Simon reached for the sponge, his hand brushing against hers. "Here," he said.

For a moment, they worked in silence, their frustration simmering beneath the surface. Angie watched him scrub at the pan, her breath catching as the tension between them shifted. The familiar comfort of being close to him, of working side by side, slowly began to seep in.

"Use a little more soap," Angie muttered, her voice shaky. "No. You need hot water, like hot."

Simon turned the water hotter, but it surprised him, and a spray of water and bubbles splashed over both of them. Angie gasped, wiping her face as Simon laughed, the sound breaking through the tension for just a moment.

They stood there, drenched and breathing heavily, staring at each other. Without a word, Angie turned on her heel, stomping toward the bedroom. She reached for the curtain that served as a makeshift door, yanking it to close off the space. But the rod gave way, the curtain falling to the floor in a heap.

Angie froze, her breath catching in her throat as she stared at the fallen curtain. Simon stood on the other side of the room, watching her, neither of them sure what to do.

There was no more space between them, no room to hide.

Simon sighed, drying his hands on a towel as he walked over to her. He bent down, picking up the curtain rod and gently placing it back up. "I'm not lying to you, Ang," his voice filled with sincerity.

Angie stood frozen, her heart pounding in her chest as he turned to walk back toward the kitchen. But before he could get far, she reached out, grabbing his hand and pulling him toward her.

Without hesitation, they kissed, desperate, passionate, like they had both been starving for the connection they had lost. It was filled with everything they hadn't said to each other, every emotion they'd kept bottled up. They had missed each other, and in that moment, nothing else mattered.

Twenty-Four

Between Fear and Hope

The bedside lamp bathed the small studio apartment in a golden light, casting gentle shadows across the walls. Angie lay next to Simon, their bodies wrapped around each other in the warmth of post-love making stillness. Her head rested against his chest, listening to the rhythmic rise and fall of his breathing. For a moment, everything felt peaceful, the storm of their lives quieted, if only for a little while.

Simon's fingers trailed absently through her hair as he whispered, "I love you."

Angie closed her eyes, letting the words sink in. "I love you too," she murmured, but there was a tension under the surface, a worry that gnawed at her, even in this brief moment of calm.

Her mind drifted to the pills, to the endless cycle they had been caught in since the accident. She didn't want to ruin the peace between them, but the question had been hanging in the air for too long, and she couldn't ignore it any longer.

"What if you tried new doctors?" Angie asked hesitantly, her fingers tracing small patterns on his chest.

Simon shifted slightly, pulling her closer but sensing the change in her tone. "What do you mean?" he asked, his voice tinged with wariness.

Angie propped herself up on her elbow, looking down at him. "You're on my insurance now," she said, her eyes searching his face. "What if you finally got a new doctor? Has your doctor done any tests recently? Like... really checked you out?"

Simon let out a sigh, his eyes drifting away from hers. "They just did the x-ray when I crashed my street bike," he muttered.

Angie frowned, a small crease forming between her brows. "That's it?" she asked, her voice incredulous. "No other tests? No follow-up? Like another x-ray or an MRI?"

Simon shook his head. "No," he admitted.

Angie sat up fully now, her annoyance bubbling beneath the surface. "Don't you think they should?" she asked, her voice filled with both concern and determination. "Maybe it's time to try something else? Unless you want to stay... your kind of normal."

Simon knew she was right, but the idea of going through more tests, more doctors, more uncertainty, felt exhausting. He ran a hand over his face, letting out a slow breath. "I don't," he said finally, his voice low. "I think that's a good idea... but there's probably no quick fix."

Angie's heart softened at his admission. "But maybe something or someone different could help you," she said, her voice quieter now, filled with hope she wasn't sure she was allowed to have.

"Maybe," Simon whispered, though the uncertainty still lingered in his eyes.

Twenty-Five

Truth of the Matter

The air in the St. Francis Church Hall was thick with the scent of coffee and faint echoes of whispered prayers. Easter decorations hung on the walls, pastel eggs and bunny cutouts adding a strange contrast to the somber atmosphere. The small group of people gathered in the room was mostly women, seated in a circle with their chairs close enough to suggest intimacy but far enough to maintain personal space.

Angie sat among them, her fingers nervously twisting the hem of her sleeve as she glanced around. She had never imagined herself in a place like this, a support group for people whose lives had been touched by addiction. But here she was, feeling both like she belonged and like she didn't. The pamphlet Benjamin had given her sat in her purse like a glowing beacon. A calling card to the words she had been too afraid to say out loud until now.

At the head of the group was Father Charles, a middle-aged priest with kind eyes and a Hawaiian shirt that clashed with his Roman collar. His easy demeanor helped to lighten the mood, making the group feel less like a meeting and more like a safe place to unload the burdens everyone carried.

"Thank you for sharing, Meredith," Father Charles said, his voice gentle as he nodded to the woman who had just spoken. "I see a couple of new faces at the table tonight. No pressure, but we welcome your voices."

Angie felt the eyes of the group on her, their silent encouragement or curiosity pressing her to speak. She hesitated for a moment, her breath catching in her throat. *Can I do this? Can I really open up to strangers*?

Her voice was shaky as she finally spoke. "Hi, um... I'm Angie," she began, her eyes darting toward Father Charles. "Um, my husband is... my addict. I never thought I'd feel like I needed to be here, but I think that's normal, right? I don't know where to start?"

Father Charles gave her an encouraging nod. "It's up to you," he said. "You can share something that happened this week if that feels easier."

Angie let out a shaky breath, her fingers trembling as she gripped the arms of her chair. "This week..." she repeated, her mind racing. Where could she even begin? "This week, I've been pulling my hair out because we're short like... two hundred dollars for rent."

Her voice wavered as she spoke, the words feeling heavier than she had anticipated. It was the most she had shared in weeks, and it felt like too much and not enough at the same time.

"We're newlyweds," Angie continued, her voice cracking slightly. "It's supposed to be happy and blissful and filled with lots of sex but... it's chaos. And then some days, he's totally normal, but I'm freaking out and it's causing gray hairs to come in. Right here," she added, pointing to the top of her head with a small, sad smile. "Um... I'm scared. And nervous. And embarrassed... really confused. Sorry."

She stopped, her chest tight with emotion. It was enough. Maybe even too much. *Did I just say "lots of sex" in front of the priest?* She could feel the lump in her throat threatening to spill into tears, but she held them back, taking a deep breath to steady herself.

Father Charles gave her a warm smile. "Angie, thank you for sharing," he said, his voice filled with compassion. "Anyone else?"

The woman seated next to Angie, a gentle-looking woman in her fifties, reached over and offered her a tissue. Angie accepted it gratefully, wiping away the tears that had begun to form in the corners of her eyes.

"You did good," the woman whispered, her voice kind. "The first one's the hardest."

Angie nodded, managing a small, shaky smile. It didn't feel like much, but for the first time in a long time, she felt like she wasn't alone. Maybe Benjamin was right, maybe it was nice to be around people who knew that crazy.

Twenty-Six

Too Close to Home

The late afternoon sun bathed Sofia's backyard in a warm, golden glow. The sound of chatter and laughter filled the air as Angie's family gathered to celebrate Tony's return and Rosie's birthday. A taco bar was spread out across the table, the smells of sizzling carne asada and freshly made tortillas mixing with the sweetness of Orange Tampico and the bitterness of Modello. The yard was too small for horseshoes, but that didn't stop the guys—Simon, Edgar, and Tony—from playing, their competitive shouts echoing across the yard.

Colorful banners hung from the fence, one welcoming Tony home from his deployment, the other wishing Rosie a happy birthday. The scene felt like home. It was familiar, comforting, and filled with the warmth of family.

Angie stood by the kitchen counter, mixing a round of margaritas with Rosie. She watched her sister out of the corner of her eye, trying to absorb some of Rosie's ease and confidence. It had been a long time since they'd had a moment to talk, just the two of them.

"Ok, here you go," Angie said, handing a glass to her mom, Sofia. "Not too strong and plenty of salt."

Sofia took the glass with a grateful smile. "Thank you, *mijitas*," she said, her voice warm as she sipped from the glass.

Rosie, with a conspiratorial smile, nudged Angie. "Grab your glass," she said, motioning with her head for Angie to follow her.

Angie hesitated but followed Rosie down the hall, to the little alcove that once served as their study desk and had now become Sofia's reading corner. The sounds of laughter and family faded as they entered the space, a quiet stillness replacing the buzz of the party outside. The room hadn't changed much, the desk they all used had been replaced by a comfy lounge chair and soft lighting but the scent of old wood and memories lingered in the air.

Rosie, turning to Angie with that familiar look of concern that only a sister could give. "Finally," she said, setting her glass down on a side table. "So, what's going on? How are you?"

Angie shrugged, trying to seem casual. "I'm good. Things are fine."

Rosie gave her a pointed look. "I'm only here for like a day," she said, her voice cutting through the pretense. "How *are* you?"

Angie, suddenly feeling exposed. "I'm ok. Really, I'm ok," she insisted, her voice a little too tight.

Rosie crossed her arms, her eyes narrowing. "You think I don't know what's going on? We all know, Ang. We can *see* him, you know. You try and hide it in your voice, but I can hear it."

Angie's chest tightened, the truth of Rosie's words pressing down on her. She dropped her gaze, fiddling with the edge of her shirt. "Some days he can function," she admitted, "and others... he's a total wreck. And then I'm a wreck."

Rosie's face filled with concern, but her words were blunt. "That's junkie behavior," she said, her voice steady.

Angie flinched at the word. Junkie. It felt too harsh, too final. "I guess," she whispered, not willing to fully admit it.

Rosie's eyes searched Angie's face, her expression serious. "You can't live like that forever," she said, her voice filled with a tough kind of love.

Angie's heart ached, but she forced a smile. "Things can get better," she said, though even she didn't fully believe it.

Rosie shook her head, her voice laced with realism. "They probably won't, though."

Angie looked away, biting her lip to stop the tears that threatened to spill. "Rosie, I'm trying to be positive," she said, her voice trembling slightly.

"And I'm realistic," Rosie replied firmly. "He's a loser, Ang. Just cut your losses. He can be like a starter marriage."

The words hit Angie hard, and she snapped her gaze back to Rosie. "No!" she said, her voice louder than she intended. "I didn't get married to give up so quickly."

Rosie sighed, shaking her head. "So what then, Ang? You're a martyr now?"

Angie's frustration bubbled up. "No," she said, her voice cracking. "I'm just... I'm just trying to figure this shit out."

Rosie didn't back down. "You deserve better, that's all."

Before Angie could respond, Rosie's phone rang, the shrill sound breaking the tension between them. Rosie glanced at the screen and turned giddy. "I gotta take this; it's Julio," she said, stepping toward the door.

Angie clenched her jaw, the frustration still simmering beneath the surface. "Whatever," she muttered under her breath, turning away as Rosie left the room.

As she walked back toward the party, Angie ran into her father, Edgar, coming down the hall.

"Angie, *mija*," he said, giving her a small smile. "I'm getting ready to go."

Angie frowned, glancing toward the backyard where the party was still in full swing. "Why, Dad? We haven't done the piñata yet."

Edgar chuckled. "I know, but I'm tired. And Gladys is waiting for me at home."

Angie searched his face, sensing something deeper in his words. "You alright?" She asked gently.

Edgar sighed, rubbing the back of his neck. "Sometimes these family things make me think," he said, his voice quiet.

"About what, Dad?" Angie asked, her heart sinking a little.

Edgar hesitated for a moment before speaking, his voice thick with emotion. "Your mom and I... we should've tried harder. Maybe she did, and I didn't. I don't know. But promise me," he said, his eyes locking onto hers, "you use all the *ganas* you got and fight for each other."

Angie blinked, her throat tightening as her father's words sank in. "You give good advice, Dad," she said. "Just like Mom."

Edgar smiled, his eyes glistening. "*Porque sabemos*," he whispered, his voice filled with a quiet wisdom that only came with age and regret.

Before the moment could linger too long, Tony and Simon came down the hallway, followed by a small entourage of family members. Tony clapped a hand on Edgar's shoulder, grinning. "Hey, Pop! Before you go, *Tia* Maya wants a family picture."

Tia Maya's voice rang out from the living room, "Come on, everyone! Gather around." *Click, click, click*, goes the wind of the disposable Kodak camera in hand.

The family began piling into the small space, squeezing together on the worn couch and kneeling on the floor to fit into the narrow viewfinder of a disposable Kodak camera.

"Edgar! Angelina! Rosie! Sofia!" *Tia* Maya called out, motioning everyone to gather closer.

Rosie joined the group with a sigh, and the room filled with the sound of shuffling bodies and playful banter.

Tony nudged Angie with a grin. "Wow, you've gotten shorter," he teased.

"Shut up," Angie muttered, elbowing him in the side.

After the picture, Tony's voice boomed out, "After this, it's *piñata* time!"

The kids cheered, Simon among them, his smile finally reaching his eyes for the first time all day.

Tia Maya held up the camera again, calling out, "Okay, ready, set, say '*Piñata*'!"

"*Piñata*!" Everyone shouted in unison, laughter echoing through the room as the camera clicked.

As the family moved to the backyard for the piñata, Simon caught Angie's eye, tapping his wrist as if to say, *It's time.* Angie's heart sank a little, the happiness of the day was fleeting too quickly.

TWENTY-SEVEN

BENEATH THE SURFACE

The newly constructed home was sleek and modern, every detail polished and deliberate. The contrast to Angie and Simone's tiny studio was as bright as the oversized windows. But despite the beauty of the space, the atmosphere felt cold and stiff. The tension was simmering just beneath the surface of polite conversation.

Angie sat on the large sofa. She crossed her legs and leaned forward, trying not to sink too far into the plushness. Across the room, Simon sat at the kitchen island with his parents. The distance between them, though small, felt immense.

Susan's voice broke the silence. "I'm glad you made it," she said, her tone neutral, but the underlying meaning hung in the air.

Simon gave a half-hearted smile, his posture stiff. "Why wouldn't we?"

Hank cleared his throat, sensing the tension but unsure how to ease it. "Your mom's just saying it's nice to have the family together," he said, his voice a little too cheerful.

Jared, Simon's older brother, was seasoning ribs with a precision that matched his methodical nature. "So, Si," Jared said, glancing over his shoulder, "how's the car business?"

Simon exhaled through his nose, keeping his voice even. "The car audio installation industry is fine."

Jared shrugged as he turned back to the ribs. "What'cha gonna do once you outgrow that crap?"

Before Simon could respond, Susan chimed in, her voice soft but pointed. "There's always school, if you apply yourself."

Simon felt the familiar frustration rising in his chest, but he kept his tone measured. "I don't know," he said, his fingers tapping lightly on the counter. "I haven't thought about it. School's never been my thing."

Jared, always the golden boy, didn't let up. "Bro, you're too smart to do that car stuff. Look at me; I got my degree in engineering. I finally got a good state job and now a house."

Simon's jaw tightened, the words stinging more than they should have. "That's what we're celebrating," he muttered under his breath.

Angie, sensing Simon's frustration, decided to step in. "Simon's been thinking about trade school," she offered, trying to bridge the gap.

Hank perked up at the suggestion, nodding thoughtfully. "A trade would be good for you. I can see that," he said, his voice filled with fatherly approval that never seemed to come easily.

Simon, eager to shift the conversation, glanced over at Jared. "How are those ribs coming?"

Jared grinned, pleased to show off his grilling skills. "All done," he said, lifting the platter with pride. "Let's throw them on the barbie. Did you see the Q Mom and Dad got me? It's sa-weet! Come on, let's light her up!"

As Jared headed out to the backyard, Simon couldn't help but feel the familiar pang of resentment. He'd never measure up to Jared in their parents' eyes. No matter what he did, he was always the one who fell short.

Susan's voice cut through his thoughts. "Simon," she said, her tone sharp, "if you get off those pills, you could actually do something. Like a trade school. You're not going to keep a real job if you're high all the time."

The words hit Simon like a slap, but he kept his expression neutral. "You're right, Mom," he said flatly. "That's why I quit. No job to keep."

Hank's face darkened. "Are you serious?"

Simon stood up from the kitchen island, his movements tense. "Serious as a moth fly," he said, his voice dripping with sarcasm.

Susan and Hank exchanged a glance, their concern deepening. Susan turned her gaze to Angie, her eyes filled with quiet judgment. "Did you know about this?"

Angie shook her head. "No," she admitted. It was news to her too.

Susan's voice grew sharper. "Look at you, Simon," she said, her frustration spilling over. "You're no good to anyone like this. Not to yourself. Not to your wife."

"We're just trying to talk some sense into you," Hank added, his voice firm but not unkind.

Simon had heard enough. He stood up from the stool, the tension in his body radiating with every step. "Why?" he said, his voice rising. "Your golden boy is out there, so you don't have to worry about me."

Hank's patience was thinning. "Your pain doesn't match the pills, son. Don't you think there's something wrong there?"

Simon's fists clenched at his sides as he walked toward the front door, filled with frustration. "I'm sorry you don't believe me," he said, his voice thick with emotion. "That I'm in pain, that sitting on these stupid wooden stools hurts my ass! It's just a bad excuse for you, I get it. And yes, it's my fault for crashing that goddamn bike you told me not to get."

Susan's concern breaking through the tension. "We want you to get help, honey," she said, her eyes pleading. "We all want to see you do better. That's all."

Simon's hand hovered over the doorknob, his back to his parents. "Yeah, well, I'm trying," he muttered before pushing open the door and walking out.

Angie hurried after Simon, grabbing her bag as she passed the kitchen island. Her heart was racing, a mix of frustration and worry gnawing at her. She paused for a moment, glancing back at Susan and Hank, who watched her with weary eyes.

"I'm sorry," Angie said quietly, her voice barely audible above the tension in the room.

Susan slid a small potted cactus across the island toward Angie. "Here, dear," she said gently. "A housewarming gift for you."

Angie blinked, momentarily caught off guard by the gesture. "Thank you," she said, her voice thick with emotion.

Susan gave her a small smile. "It's low maintenance," she added.

Angie nodded, clutching the little cactus as she followed Simon out the door.

By the time Angie caught up to Simon, he was already at the car, leaning against the passenger door with his arms crossed. His eyes were distant, the anger from the argument still simmering beneath the surface.

Angie unlocked the doors and slid into the driver's seat, glancing over at him as he climbed in beside her.

"Hey," Angie said. "What was that about? No more blowing her off?"

Simon let out a bitter laugh, shaking his head. "Did you see that barbecue they got him?"

Angie frowned, glancing over at him. "So?"

Simon's jaw tightened as he looked out the window. "He's always been their favorite," he said, the bitterness in his voice undeniable.

Angie reached over, placing her hand on his arm. "Cause he's vanilla," she said. "You can always count on vanilla."

Simon turned to look at her, a flicker of emotion crossing his face. "It's not fair."

Angie sighed, her heart aching for him. "What? That they love you and care for you?"

"I'm trying, Angie," Simon said, his voice raw. "I'm always trying."

Angie's hand tightened on his arm, her voice gentle. "I know," she said, her heart breaking a little at the vulnerability in his words. "Babe, you're like chocolate malted crunch. You're all kinds of sensations."

Simon let out a small, surprised laugh, the tension between them easing just a little. "What's that?" he asked, pointing to the small cactus on the dashboard.

Angie glanced at it and smiled. "Our housewarming gift," she said with a hint of amusement.

Simon snorted. "Figures," he muttered. "I'm not going back in there," he added, his voice firm. "They don't get me. I just keep letting them down. Fuck it. So, now what?"

Angie sighed, her mind racing as she tried to think of a way to lighten the moment. "I don't know," she said, her voice quiet. "I think we need some fun. Like real, get outta Dodge fun. We should plan a road trip."

Simon turned to her, his eyes sparking with the same wild idea. "Or we could go right now."

"Sure." she said, "Why not?" her voice filled with sudden excitement.

Simon excitedly shares the plan, "I'm serious. We stop at home, five minutes to pack and we're out."

The door to the tiny studio apartment flew open. Angie and Simon rushed inside, their hearts racing with the thrill of their sudden decision. The apartment felt like a momentary stop on the way to something bigger, something that, for just a little while, would let them forget everything.

Angie grabbed clothes and tossed them into a medium-sized duffle bag with little care for what matched. Simon scooped up their toiletries from the bathroom counter, shoving them into the bag with the same reckless urgency. It wasn't about packing perfectly. It was about the escape.

Within minutes, they were done, their bags slung over their shoulders as they darted back out the door, laughing at the rush of it all. The apartment door clicked shut behind them, leaving behind their routine, their worries, and the arguments that seemed to follow them everywhere.

Twenty-Eight

Not Everything's a Disaster

The coastal roads stretched out before them, the open highway leading them south, away from everything they knew. The rhythmic sound of the tires against the pavement seemed to pause the tension that had been building between them for weeks. With the windows down, the cool night air rushed in, filling the car with the scent of saltwater and freedom.

Angie sat in the passenger seat, her hand hanging out the window, playing with the wind. Her fingers danced through the air as she watched the lights of Malibu and Santa Monica blur by. There was a peace in the moment, a quiet joy in the simplicity of being together, driving with no real destination in mind.

Simon drove with one hand on the wheel, his other hand resting on Angie's leg. He glanced over at her, watching her smile softly as the wind tangled her hair. For the first time in a long while, he felt a lightness, a feeling that had been missing in the day-to-day grind of pain and frustration.

But then, Simon's voice broke the peaceful silence, his tone a little too casual, as if he were trying to ease into something uncomfortable. "I didn't quit my job," he admitted, his eyes focused on the road ahead. "They let me go."

Angie's smile faded as she turned to him, her hand dropping from the window. "When?" she asked, her voice cautious, already bracing for the answer.

Simon shrugged, his fingers tapping the steering wheel. "Like a few days ago."

Angie frowned, a knot tightening in her chest. "What's 'a few?'" she pressed, sensing there was more to the story.

Simon hesitated, his grip tightening on the wheel. "Like... last week."

"Simon Alexander! Shit," Angie cursed, sitting up straighter in her seat. The knot in her chest grew tighter, frustration bubbling up inside her. "Why didn't you tell me?"

Simon let out a sigh, his eyes flicking toward her before returning to the road. "I didn't want to worry you," he muttered. "I already got another gig."

Angie raised an eyebrow, her skepticism clear. "How?"

Simon smiled, that easy confidence slipping back into his voice. "You know Freddy? He's got a cousin at a supermarket warehouse, they've been looking for someone" he explained. "I'll be a machine maintenance guy."

Angie couldn't help but laugh, shaking her head. "Only you could have things fall into your lap like that," she teased, her frustration melting away in the face of Simon's ability to always land on his feet.

Simon grinned, giving her a playful look. "I like it when *you* fall in my lap," he said, his voice low and teasing.

Angie blushed, a small smile tugging at her lips despite herself. There was something about Simon's charm, something she could never quite resist.

Simon reached over and took her hand, bringing it to his lips for a quick kiss. "It's better pay too," he said, his voice lighter now as the lingering tension had lifted. "What can I say? I'm a straight baller up in here."

Angie snorted, rolling her eyes but unable to suppress her smile. "Tru dat," she quipped, their banter a welcomed reprieve.

The night wore on, giving way to the slower pace of the coastal towns, the highway stretching out before them like a promise of something different. Hours passed, and eventually, the familiar signs of the Tijuana border came into view. Simon and Angie exchanged a glance, the excitement of the unknown sparking between them.

Crossing into Mexico felt like stepping into another world. The lights of Rosarito lit up the night, the streets alive with music, laughter, and the smell of street tacos. The vibrant energy of the town was infectious, pulling Angie and Simon into its rhythm.

They parked the car and stepped out into the night, the sounds of the clubs reverberated around them. Angie felt a giddy kind of freedom, her earlier worries fading as she took Simon's hand and led him toward the bustling taco stands.

They grabbed street tacos from a vendor, the fresh salsa and warm tortillas filling the air with mouth watering aromas. Simon handed her a glass-bottled Modelo, and they wandered through the open-air market, eating and drinking as they soaked in the atmosphere.

The tension from earlier had evaporated, replaced by a sense of playfulness they hadn't felt in months. It was just the two of them. No expectations, no pressure. Just the joy of being together in the moment.

They found their way into an open-air bar, the music pulsing around them as they took seats at the bar. The bartender poured them shots of tequila, and Simon clinked his glass against Angie's, his eyes twinkling with mischief.

"To us," he said, his voice filled with a mix of hope and determination.

Angie raised her glass, meeting his gaze. "To us," she echoed, her heart swelling with a mixture of love and uncertainty. As they downed the shots, the familiar burn of the alcohol made Angie laugh, her cheeks flushed from both the drink and the excitement of the night.

The bar was a little more than a makeshift structure, with four flimsy walls encasing a small patch of sand and a wooden plank dance floor that creaked underfoot. It wasn't glamorous, but it had a certain raw charm. Unpolished and perfectly suited to their spontaneous adventure. The bartender, an older man with sun-worn skin, flipped the cassette in the boom box, and the familiar synth beats of 80's music filled the air.

Simon and Angie were the only ones on the dance floor, the sand beneath them crunching as they swayed to the rhythm. The air was cool, the night sky above clear and dotted with stars, and for a moment, everything outside the walls of this bar felt distant, like a world far away from the one they were creating here.

Angie glanced over at Simon, her heart swelling with affection and concern. She leaned in closer, her voice gentle as she spoke, "I think a new job is good for you," she said, her words carrying hope. "I don't think those installs were helping your issues."

Simon nodded, his eyes on the horizon, but there was a flicker of doubt in his expression. "I should've left a while ago," he admitted, the realization settling in as he said the words out loud.

"Change is good, right?" Angie continued, her hand resting lightly on his arm. "New doctor, new job... it's time." She smiled, trying to reassure him, but she could feel the tension in his body, the way his shoulders tightened ever so slightly.

Simon let out a small sigh, his voice quieter now. "Change makes me nervous, though."

Angie tilted her head, searching his face. "Why?" she asked gently.

"Because it's like you're losing control," Simon said, his voice strained with the vulnerability he rarely let show. "You make changes hoping things will be okay, but you never really know."

Angie nodded, understanding the fear that came with letting go of the familiar, even when the familiar wasn't good. "That's why we have faith," she said, her voice filled with quiet wisdom. "We cling to what we know and hope it's enough to carry us through."

"Yeah," Simon muttered, his eyes dropping to the ground.

"I know," Simon said, his voice barely above a whisper. "I just...I don't like losing my comfort zone."

Angie took a deep breath. "Things have to change," she said, her eyes locked with his. "We won't make it if you don't get better."

There was a pause, the air between them thick with unspoken fear. But then Simon gestured toward the bar, a mischievous smile tugging at his lips. "Ha, check that out," he said, breaking the tension.

Angie followed his gaze, squinting up at the ceiling of the bar. "G-strings?" she asked, laughing as she saw the clothesline above the bar, strung with colorful, patron-donated G-strings swaying lightly in the night breeze.

Simon grinned, the playfulness returning to his eyes. "You wanna give 'em yours?"

Angie smirked, shaking her head. "I would, but I wore my granny panties tonight."

Simon chuckled, pulling her closer to him. "Figures," he teased, pressing a gentle kiss to her forehead.

The night was quiet but for the gentle sound of the waves crashing against the shore. Their motel room, though modest, sat right on the beach, and the moonlight cast a beautiful shimmer over the ocean.

Angie stood on the small balcony, her arms resting on the railing as she gazed out at the vastness of the sea. The cool breeze tugged at her hair, and for a moment, she let herself get lost in the rhythmic lull of the ocean, the sounds grounding her in the present.

Simon stepped onto the balcony, wrapping his arms around her waist from behind. His chin rested on her head as he pulled her into his warmth, then kissed her neck. They stood there in silence for a moment, both knowing that this peace between them was fragile but beautiful in its simplicity.

"I know I'm not who I want to be yet," Simon murmured, his breath warm against her skin. "But I'm trying to get there."

Angie turned in his arms, her hands resting gently on his chest as she looked up at him. His face was filled with vulnerability. The walls he usually kept up were lowered. "I know," she said. "I can see him like you can see me." Her voice quivered slightly as she recalled her own struggles. The days when she had hidden behind baggy clothes and self-doubt, not feeling good enough, not feeling worthy. "Remember? When I was hiding, not feeling good about being me?"

Simon lovingly brushed a strand of hair away from her face. "Baby, you've always been fly," he said with a gentle smile. "How could you not see it?"

Angie laughed, shaking her head. "No, I ain't no pin-up girl."

Simon's expression grew serious, his voice filled with conviction. "You're more than that, Angelina. You are. You're a rare breed."

It was always different with Angie. "I. Love. You," he said, each word deliberate, filled with the emotion he struggled to express. He didn't have to wear the mask or be anything more or less than exactly who he was. Broken, unsure, still figuring it out, but safe. She saw all of him.

Angie smiled, her heart full. "Show me," she whispered, her voice barely audible as she leaned closer to him.

Simon's smile widened, the playful glint returning to his eyes. "Yes ma'am," he murmured, his lips brushing against hers.

They kissed passionately, the intensity of their connection filling the space between them. Simon backed her up toward the sliding glass door, his hands roaming over her back as they stumbled, laughing, against the glass.

With a breathless laugh, Angie slid the door open, and they tumbled inside, their energy shifting from playful to urgent. Simon's hands moved to undress her, his fingers tugging at her shirt as she reached for his, pulling it over his head.

Angie stepped out of her jeans, revealing her sexy, cute lace underwear, the humor of their earlier conversation not lost on either of them.

"I knew you weren't wearing granny panties!" Simon teased, his voice filled with laughter as they collapsed onto the bed, their laughter mingling with the sound of the ocean just outside.

Under the moonlit sky, everything else fell away. It was just the two of them. Just love, and the quiet promise of trying, no matter how difficult it got.

Twenty-Nine

Good Morning, Panic!

The room was quiet, the faint sound of waves lapping against the shore just audible through the slightly open window. Angie stirred in bed, her arm reaching out instinctively, only to find the space beside her empty. She blinked groggily, her heart sinking as her hand patted the empty sheets where Simon should have been.

"Simon?" she called out, her voice still thick with sleep. She sat up, rubbing her eyes and scanning the small motel room. "Simon?" she called again, louder this time, but there was no answer.

Her heart began to race, worry creeping in as she glanced around the room. His clothes were gone, his shoes missing from the floor. She swung her legs over the side of the bed, her mind racing as she grabbed her jeans and pulled them on in a hurry.

"Are you freakin' kidding me?" she muttered under her breath, throwing on a shirt as she rushed toward the door. Panic was bubbling up inside her, but she pushed it down, trying to stay calm.

Angie yanked open the motel room door and peered down the hallway. Nothing. Stepping out into the cool morning air, scanning the empty stretch of the motel parking lot. Still no Simon. Her hands shook as she pulled out her phone, dialing his number. It rang once, then twice, but went straight to voicemail. She tried again, her frustration mounting as it went to voicemail once more.

"Dammit, Simon," she hissed, punching the air in frustration. She stood there for a moment, her breath coming in shallow gasps as she tried to calm the rising tide of fear and anger. *Where the hell are you?*

The streets of Rosarito were quiet, the early morning sun casting long shadows over the gravel roads. Simon strolled leisurely down the street, his hands shoved into his pockets as he glanced at the vendors setting up their stalls for the day. The world seemed peaceful here.

He ducked into a small *panadería*, the smell of freshly baked sweet bread filling the air. The woman behind the counter greeted him with a smile, and Simon ordered two cups of coffee and a couple of *conchas*. As he stepped back out onto the street, he spotted a scruffy-looking man sitting curbside, a makeshift artist with a scattering of canvases and brushes at his feet.

Simon crouched down beside the man, handing him one of the cups of coffee and a piece of bread. The man looked up, his eyes tired but grateful as he accepted the small offering.

They exchanged a few words, casual pleasantries about the weather and the quiet of the morning.

Simon stood up again and continued down a side street. He paused in front of a modest building, the sign above the door reading *"Dr. Muñoz."* His hand hovered over the doorknob for a moment before he pushed it open and stepped inside.

Back in the motel room, Angie paced the floor, her fingers twisting anxiously around the hem of her shirt. She had been sitting on the edge of the bed, biting her nails, waiting. But waiting wasn't something she could do anymore. Every minute that passed without Simon brought a fresh wave of panic.

She had been here before, wondering where he was, wondering what he was doing, and if he was okay. This wasn't new. And yet, every time it happened, it felt like a fresh wound being reopened.

Her phone buzzed in her hand, but it wasn't Simon. Just a message from work. She sighed, tossing the phone onto the bed as she sank down onto the edge of it, her foot tapping restlessly against the floor.

The anxious silence gnawed at her. Simon had been gone for what felt like hours, and though she knew better than to panic right away, it didn't stop the worry from growing. Her phone sat next to her, mocking her with its stillness, her calls to him unanswered.

Then her thoughts drifted back to when she saw him just after his accident. Before his pain and the pills had become a part of their routine, before everything had grown so complicated. If only they had known they were standing on the edge of darkness.

Thirty

Blissfully Unaware

The Wagner home had always felt both familiar and uncomfortable for Angie. As she knocked on the front door that evening, part of her was nervous about seeing Simon after the accident, but another part of her still felt drawn to him in ways she couldn't explain.

Jared answered the door, his usual easy going demeanor intact despite everything. "Oh hey, Ang," he said, stepping aside to let her in. "I'm glad you got my message."

She hesitated for a moment before stepping inside, offering Jared a small smile as she took in the warm, homey atmosphere. Susan and Hank were in the dining room, setting the table for dinner. The scene felt normal considering what had happened.

"Hey Ma, look who stopped by," Jared called over his shoulder.

Susan looked up from her task, her face lighting up with genuine warmth. "Oh, Angie dear, good to see you."

Hank gave her a nod, his expression slightly more subdued. "Hello there, stranger."

"Hi," Angie replied, a bit nervously. "How are you?"

Susan shrugged, her hands smoothing over the napkins as she placed them down. "Fine. A little frazzled, I guess."

It wasn't hard to guess why. Simon's accident lingered in the air, a reminder of how close they had come to losing him.

Susan gestured toward the table. "Will you be joining us for dinner?"

Angie shook her head, her heart pounding in her chest. "Oh, no thank you. I just came by to say hi."

Hank motioned toward the stairs. "You can go on up, hon."

She nodded gratefully, her steps quick and quiet as she made her way upstairs to Simon's room. She could hear Susan's voice, as she turned the corner. "She's always been my favorite," she heard her say to Hank.

When she reached Simon's bedroom door, she hesitated for a moment, her hand hovering over the knob before she knocked gently.

"Yeah," came Simon's voice, slightly muffled from behind the door.

"Hi Simon, it's Angie," she called, pushing the door open just enough to peek inside.

Simon was lying on the bed, shirtless, wearing nothing but a pair of sweatpants. His movements were slow, labored, and every small shift in position seemed to bring a grimace to his face. Still, when he saw her, a crooked smile appeared.

"Hey," he said, trying to sit up.

"Hey," Angie replied, stepping inside and closing the door behind her.

For a moment, they just looked at each other. The awkwardness of not knowing how to act in this new space between them was evident. Angie's eyes trailed over Simon, searching for signs of the damage she knew the accident had caused. "You okay?" she asked, her voice filled with concern.

Simon let out a dry chuckle. "Well, I mean, I'm not dead," he said, wincing as he moved. "But my bike is trashed."

Angie, not sure how to respond to his nonchalance. "And you're hurt?" she asked, her eyes scanning him for visible injuries.

Simon motioned to his desk as he slowly stood up with a nod. "Look over there."

Angie walked over and picked up his riding leathers, stiff with grime and torn in several places. The scratches and gashes in the leather told a story of impact, of friction, of a body thrown against the pavement. Beside the leathers were large prescription bottles of Vicodin and another bottle of Somas.

"Holy shit," she whispered, her eyes wide as she took it all in. "That's... you could've..."

"Yep," Simon cut her off, trying to downplay it. "Damn things saved my life, want to see." He turned around, wincing as he did, and then dropped his sweatpants to show her the deep bruising that spread across the back of his left hip and down his thigh.

His skin was an ugly shade of the deepest purple and black, the kind of bruise that made her stomach turn. "Oh my God," she whispered, horrified. "That's disgusting."

Simon chuckled, though the laugh was strained. "What? It's not sexy?"

"Roadkill isn't sexy," she shot back, trying to mask her concern. "There's like a quarter of you that's dead." Angie leaned in to inspect the bruising. Disgusted, yet oddly fascinated.

"Ahem. Commando, I see?" she smirked as she stood. "Yep, bare minimum," Simon smirked back.

Simon struggled to reach down and pull his pants back up, wincing in pain with each movement. Without thinking, Angie stepped forward, kneeling down to help him. Her fingers brushed against his skin as she pulled the fabric over the bruised area, her heart aching at the sight of him so vulnerable and almost naked.

"You in pain?" she asked, looking up at him.

Simon sighed, nodding toward the bottles on the desk. "Yeah. Feels like I got hit by a Mack truck, but those help." He gestured toward the pills, his voice trailing off awkwardly. "So... it's been a little while."

"Yeah," Angie replied. "I hope it's okay that I came by."

"Of course," Simon said. He looked at her with an intensity that made her heart skip a beat. He reached out, taking her hand in his. They just stood there for a moment, pretending that the distance between them could somehow mask the spark that had always been there.

"I'm glad you're okay," Angie said quietly, her voice barely above a whisper.

Then they spoke at the same time, their words overlapping in the small space between them.

"I'm gonna get going," Angie started, but Simon interrupted with a quiet, "Will you hang for a bit?"

Angie hesitated, her mind warring with her heart. "So, you have a near-death experience, and now you want me around?" she asked, her voice tinged with both bitterness and affection.

Simon smirked, shrugging slightly. "I have a near-death experience, and you run to me?" he countered, his tone playful despite the tension between them.

He leaned in, his lips inches from hers, but Angie pulled back, her heart tinged with guilt. "I'm kind of seeing someone," she admitted, her voice barely above a whisper.

Simon looked at her, his eyes searching hers. "You could've just called," he said with a sly grin, as he made another attempt to close the distance between them.

Angie shook her head, her heart pounding. "I feel like I'm cheating somebody," she confessed, her hands resting on his bare chest as if to keep herself grounded.

"What does your heart want?" Simon asked, his voice low as he reached up to gently hold her hand against his chest.

Angie's fingers tapped against his skin, her mind racing. "We can take things slow," Simon offered, his tone hopeful.

But Angie shook her head again. "We're way past that, Simon," she said, her voice firm. "I'm not doing this on and off thing again. I better go."

She turned to leave, but Simon tugged at her hand, stopping her in her tracks. "I'm sorry I hurt you, Angie," he said, his voice filled with sincerity. "You were right. I've been scared or whatever. But... I've really missed you."

Angie's eyes met his. "Why?"

Simon smiled, his voice tender. "Cause, you know, you're the salt to my pepper, baby."

Angie let out a laugh, shaking her head. "I need more than you being cute, Si."

Simon took a deep breath, his eyes serious now. "I don't do romance," he admitted, his voice vulnerable.

Angie smirked. "Oh, you can try," she teased.

Simon shrugged, searching for the right words. "I mean... I don't know," he started, stumbling over his thoughts. "I guess... when you're not around, my days don't make sense. And I thought I didn't want to feel this way again, but the truth is,

I've never felt *this* way... I don't know. You're what's right for me, Angie. I've missed you making things make sense."

Angie's heart fluttered, her resolve weakening. "See, now that was a nice start," she said. "But what does that mean?"

Simon stepped closer, his voice dropping to a low, sincere tone. "You know what that means."

Angie shook her head slightly, her voice laced with a mix of frustration and vulnerability. "Do I? 'Cause you've had a really shitty way of showing it, Si."

He held her gaze, his eyes steady and full of something deeper than the usual playful charm. "Angelina, I love you. I'm sorry... and I love you."

There was something in his tone, unguarded and raw, that melted the last of the defenses she had been holding onto. Her lips curved into a small, teasing smile. "So what? We do this grown-up style? Lock it down with a chain?"

Simon smiled, stepping even closer as his hand found hers. "Around my heart, sugar."

This time, when Simon leaned in to kiss her, she didn't pull away. She let him.

Thirty-One

Reality, My Annoying Friend

The memory faded as the sound of a key in the lock jolted Angie back to the present. She shot up from the edge of the bed, her heart pounding in her chest. The door creaked open, and there he was, Simon, strolling in like he hadn't just disappeared for hours.

Angie felt a surge of frustration, her stomach churning with the familiar cocktail of worry and anger. "What the hell, Simon?" she snapped, her words harsher than she intended.

Simon, clearly not sober and looking far too pleased with himself, held up two poorly wrapped square packages in his hands. "That's not very nice," he slurred, his eyes glassy. "Look what I bought us."

Angie took a step forward, incredulous. "Where have you been? I woke up, and you were gone. You didn't leave a note, your phone was off... I didn't know where you were." Her voice wavered between anger and fear, the sinking feeling of dread still in her gut.

Simon just blinked, as if her panic hadn't even registered. "Why? What'd you think happened?" he asked with a casual shrug, like he didn't understand the gravity of it.

"I don't know, something not good," she said, her voice tight, frustration turning into exhaustion.

He waved her off like it was nothing, lifting the packages toward her. "I was just walking around. I met a guy who's an artist. Look what I got for us!"

He pulled back the flimsy paper to reveal two paintings; crude, colorful images of breasts. Angie stared at them, her mouth slightly open, her mind scrambling to understand what she was looking at. "They're... boobs," she finally said.

Simon grinned. "Yeah, nice, right?"

Angie felt the anger creeping back in, mixing with disbelief. "Why do we need paintings of boobies, Simon?"

"Why not?" he said, completely unfazed. "I thought they'd look nice in our place."

A sarcastic laugh escaped her. "Yeah, perfect over the kitchen table."

Simon frowned, his voice dropping a little. "You could say 'thank you.'"

Angie paused, staring into his eyes, searching for the truth underneath his carefree attitude. His pupils were slightly dilated, his expression too relaxed. She sighed deeply. "Look at me," she said, her voice more serious now. She studied his face closely, her heart sinking. "What did you take?"

Simon blinked, feigning innocence. "Nothing."

"Simon..." she pressed, her tone firm. She knew the signs too well by now.

His shoulders slumped slightly, as if giving in. "I got some Somas. But don't be mad, okay?" he pleaded, his voice childish in that way that always made her heart ache, despite everything.

Angie exasperated. "We've been here less than twenty-four hours, how the hell did you find Somas?"

"I started talking to the guy with the paintings," Simon explained, oblivious to her anger. "He has a bad back too. He told me about a doctor down the street."

"Oh surprise!," she muttered. "The boobie man has a contact. How in God's name do you find these people?" The absurdity of it was almost too much.

Simon looked at her, confused by her reaction. "He's right here on the street. What's the big deal?"

Angie's eyes widened, her hands flying up in exasperation. "Oh my God. Simon, we're leaving. Right now."

He looked down at the paintings, then back up at her, as if unsure why she was so upset. "Are you mad now?"

She let out a bitter laugh, throwing her hands up in the air. "No, I'm just peachy. Let's go home."

Simon's face fell a little as he reached into his pockets, pulling out more pills. "You gonna make me get rid of these?" he asked, almost sheepishly.

Angie stared at the pills for a moment, feeling the familiar disappointment settle into her bones. "What's the point?" she said, her voice flat. "You somehow seem to pull them out of your ass."

"I told you I'm trying," he said, his tone quieter now, almost childlike in its need for reassurance.

Angie crossed her arms, her frustration giving way to a deep, exhausted sigh. "Yeah, and I'm trying not to go Jack Bauer on your ass. Let's just go."

Simon lingered for a moment, watching her, then nodded. They both knew the routine by now. The endless cycle of promises and frustrations, the night of good moments slipping away through their fingers again.

Thirty-Two

Last Call

The room had the same musty smell, but something felt different this time, emptier. Moving boxes lined the walls. Fish sat at the small table, counting out pills with slow, deliberate movements. The safe, once packed with inventory, now looked half-heartedly stocked, as if it, too, was preparing to leave.

Simon, Fish, Freddy, and Johnny sat scattered around the room, each of them quieter than usual. The banter was there, but it felt forced, a mask over something they all knew was coming.

Johnny leaned forward, tapping his foot impatiently. "So, does your liquidation sale come with a discount, fool?" he asked, trying to break the tension.

Fish didn't even look up, his voice flat. "Not for you."

Johnny scoffed, throwing his hands up. "What the hell, man? What'd I do to you?"

Fish finally looked up, a hint of amusement in his eyes. "You dated my sister, dumb ass."

"One date!" Johnny protested. "I didn't even touch her!"

Fish's lips curled into a smirk. "Exactly, man. You made her feel unwanted."

Johnny blinked, shaking his head. "Fuck. I try to be a gentleman, and it backfires."

Simon, lounging against the arm of the couch, chuckled under his breath. "That's harsh, man. Should'a been a dick. Then she would've wanted a second date."

Johnny slumped back in his seat, defeated. "I guess."

Fish's Motorola flip phone rang, cutting through the conversation. The name "TRINA" flashed across the small screen. Freddy glanced at it, then at Fish. "Hey boss, that's Trina. You want me to...?"

Fish waved him off, eyes back on the pills. "Leave it. I'll call her in a bit."

Simon with genuine concern crossing his face. "Is she doing any better?"

Fish exhaled, his eyes tired. "Physically, yeah. But mentally? Nah. She's all trippin'. I mean, I get it. She almost fuckin' died."

The room went quiet. There was an unspoken understanding between them. Each of them had danced too close to that line at one point or another. Simon felt a lump in his throat as he thought about it, his mind flicking back to his own close calls.

Fish continued, more to himself than anyone else. "Once you see that... that eyes-rolled-back shit, you know it's over. I'm done, man. That's it."

Simon's brow furrowed in disbelief. "Just like that?"

Fish nodded, his hands now still over the tray of pills. "Yeah. You can only get close to death so many times. And this neighborhood? It's changing, man. Shady fools coming by all the time. The Trina thing? That just sealed it."

He handed a tray of pills to Simon, who began quietly filling his empty prescription bottles. There was no joy in it, no excitement like there used to be. Just routine. Like filling gas in a car that could break down at any moment.

Freddy, who had been watching them both, spoke up, his voice unusually serious. "Yeah, man. Peeps are getting hooked hard now. It's not the same crowd anymore."

Fish nodded slowly, his gaze distant. "Yeah. All this shit has happened so it's like a sign you know. "Get the fuck out!"

Johnny, always one for an awkward attempt at levity, snorted. "Detox ain't no fun, man."

Fish laughed, but it was bitter. "We ain't goin' cold turkey. The ganga will help us wean off a bit."

Freddy shifted uncomfortably in his seat, his voice low. "I don't wanna be no prison bitch either. That's what happens if we keep going."

Simon looked around the room, at the faces of the men he'd spent years getting high with, laughing with, surviving with. Now, they were all talking about quitting, about moving on. It felt surreal, like the end of something they couldn't quite grasp yet.

"So you're both gonna be stand-up citizens now?" Simon asked, his voice edged with disbelief.

Freddy shrugged. "Already on my way, man. Working at my primo's body shop."

Fish, still focused on the pills, nodded. "Moving in with my pops. Gonna try to be straight and narrow. Maybe get some learning on."

Johnny, who had been quiet for too long, suddenly perked up. "Me too, man. I think I wanna be a yoga instructor."

The room fell silent as all eyes turned toward Johnny. Fish raised an eyebrow, Freddy blinked in disbelief, and Simon just stared.

Johnny threw his hands up in defense. "What? Spend all day with 'dem beautiful babies!"

Fish shook his head, smirking. "Like a fuckin' child molester. Perv."

Simon leaned forward, a grin spreading across his face. "You ain't got no game on the street, homie. You gonna genie up some magic fool?"

Freddy chuckled, shaking his head. "Man, you done broke that lamp."

Johnny glared at them all, crossing his arms. "I hate you guys."

But the laughter that followed wasn't harsh. It was familiar, easy and like old times. But even then, beneath the jokes, there was an understanding that things were changing, whether they liked it or not.

Thirty-Three

Chaos Is My Comfort Zone

The studio apartment was suffocatingly small, its once cozy atmosphere now a jumble of mess and broken promises. Simon lay reclined behind the curtain, his eyes glazed over as he scraped the last remnants of a pill onto a tile, forming neat little lines that would deliver the relief he craved. The tray, blade, and hollowed-out pen were his tools of escape, the quiet ritual that had slowly become a part of him.

With a swift motion, Simon snorted the lines and shoved the tray under the bed, retreating into the numbing void.

The front door creaked open, and Angie entered, her eyes immediately scanning the disaster around her. The pile of unfolded laundry on the futon, the dirty dishes in the sink, and the cereal bowl still sitting on the table from that morning. The sight of it all felt like an echo of their lives, slipping further and further into disorder. She sighed loudly.

"Hey babe," she muttered, her voice laced with exhaustion.

Simon, barely able to stay awake, slurred, "Howdy ho," a tired grin forming on his face.

Her patience was already threadbare. She could hear the grogginess in his voice, see the way his eyes fluttered closed, unable to stay open. This wasn't the Simon she had fallen in love with. This was someone she was beginning not to recognize.

"Thanks for cleaning up," Angie bit out, sarcasm in her tone. "Your attention to detail is impeccable."

Simon, half asleep, mumbled incoherently, "I'm... gonna clean... in a minute."

Frustration surged within her as she moved around the room, trying to figure out where to start. Every step felt like she was walking through quicksand, unable to lift the burden of their life together. She pulled back the curtain, her eyes drawn to the clutter around the bed; cups, plates, scattered laundry. She bent down and spotted something odd under the bed.

"What the hell is this?" Angie's voice was sharp as she pulled out the tray with the tile and blade.

Simon barely stirred, his eyes half-open as he mumbled, "What?"

Her pulse quickened. "What is this, Simon? Wake up!" she demanded, shaking the tray. "What the hell is this?"

Simon blinked lazily. "Oh, you know..."

"No, I don't," she snapped, her heart pounding. "Oh my God, are you doing cocaine now? Are you seriously that stupid?"

Simon laughed weakly. "You crazy, girl."

"Then what is this? What else am I supposed to think?" she cried, feeling like the ground beneath her was slipping away.

"It's not for coke," he slurred, barely managing to lift his head.

"Then what, Simon?" Her voice cracked as she threw the tray onto the bed, the blade clattering onto the mattress. "Tell me what."

"Pills," he admitted, eyes glassy.

"Pills?" Her relief was almost comical. "Oh, great. You're snorting pills. I thought it was coke. It's just pills." Her laughter was edged with hysteria. "Oh, thank God."

Angie rushed to the bathroom, gripping the sink for support, staring at her reflection. She barely recognized the woman in the mirror. Someone constantly caught between hope and despair. When she returned, her voice was steadier but strained.

"Why the hell are you snorting pills?"

Simon, barely coherent, answered simply, "Because."

"Because why?" She grabbed his arm, shaking him slightly. "Simon! Wake up, damn it. Because why?"

He groaned. "It gets to the blood stream quicker. Doesn't have to go through my tummy."

"That is so bad for you," she hissed, incredulous at his logic.

"It's gravy, baby."

Angie's heart sank as his words dripped with a casual indifference that sent a chill down her spine. "Gravy?" She let out a shaky breath. "If they wanted you to snort them, they'd put it on the label. Instead, it says 'take with food,' not 'comes with a blade.'"

"You worry too much," Simon mumbled, already fading back into his drug-induced haze.

She stood frozen for a moment, her chest tight with anger, hurt, and the growing realization that she couldn't do this anymore.

"That's it," she muttered, the words barely audible. "I'm done." Angie's hands shook as she stormed toward the closet, yanking out a large suitcase. "I can't do this shit anymore, Simon. I'm so fucking tired of all this."

Simon stirred slightly. "What? No... don't leave. I'm trying, Ang. I'm trying."

"That's all you do!" she shouted, throwing clothes into the suitcase haphazardly. "Try? At what? Failing? Well, congratulations! You've succeeded!"

She threw her arms in the air like she was cheering for him, the bitter sarcasm clear.

"You like things this way," Simon mumbled, his voice barely a whisper.

Angie froze, staring at him in disbelief. "I swear to God, Simon, I'm gonna punch you in the balls." She pointed a trembling finger at him. "This is not fun for me. I see the man I love slowly killing himself. All you got is me. Everyone else has bowed out."

Simon's response was detached. "That sounds so mean."

Her hands balled into fists as her voice cracked with frustration. "I'm sorry to hurt your feelings, Peter Pan."

Simon sat up slightly, wobbling as he shifted his pillow. "See I mess things up. You put them, parts together. It's how I jelly and you jam butter."

Angie stared at him, her mind spinning. "What?"

"I take you places that you're afraid to go," he repeated, slurring his words, "and then you save me... like Superman but you're a girl."

Simon wobbled out of bed, grabbing his pillow and shambling toward the futon. He collapsed onto the clean laundry, spreading out like a man who didn't have a care in the world.

"Here's what we'll do," he mumbled. "We'll have a trial separation. I'll sleep on the thing, you sleep there."

Angie watched in stunned silence as he made a motion like he was locking his lips and tossing away the key. In moments, Simon was snoring loudly, already lost to his own world.

She slumped onto the floor, her back against the bed. Exhaustion, frustration, and despair washed over her in waves as she hugged a throw pillow to her chest. Burying her face in it, she screamed—her voice muffled but filled with the pent up rage and sorrow of a woman trapped in a life there was no clean fix to.

Thirty-Four

Toast

The night air was thick as Simon slowly navigated the golf cart around the warehouse perimeter. His vision blurred, his thoughts fragmented, like pieces of a puzzle scattered in his mind that he couldn't quite grasp. The cart's engine was distant, almost soothing, lulling him further into the hazy abyss of his high. The darkness around the warehouse felt endless, mirroring the emptiness inside of him.

He coasted to a stop, his body slumping forward, motioning for a pedestrian that didn't exist. His head hung low, eyelids closing. His body numbed by the drugs coursing through his veins.

"Simon, what's your twenty?" The crackle of the walkie-talkie pierced through the fog in his brain, waking him just enough to register the voice of his supervisor, Bill.

Simon blinked, his mouth dry. "I'm over by the shop," he mumbled, trying to steady his voice, to sound more alert than he felt.

"Break time's up. I need you to service the freezer in building twelve," Bill's voice came again, firm but not unkind.

"You got it," Simon slurred, his hand fumbling with the cart's controls. He pushed onward toward building twelve, the cart moving with sluggish determination. The delivery door was up, an invitation to pull inside. Pallets of frozen food loomed like silent sentinels, waiting to be shipped out, waiting for someone competent to handle them.

Simon brought the cart to a stop, or tried to. His head drooped forward again as the cart rolled slowly, aimlessly, into a stack of boxes. The impact was abrupt, a soft landing, but it was enough to rattle him from his stupor for a brief second.

Minutes passed. He wasn't sure how long he had been sitting there, slumped over, feeling the numbness in his limbs. The sound of footsteps echoed in the distance before Bill rounded the corner.

"Dumb ass," Bill muttered under his breath, the words laced with frustration but not anger. He had seen this coming. "Simon, what the hell man. I've been calling you for fifteen minutes."

Simon blinked, lifting his head, trying to shake off the haze. "Oh, sorry. I didn't hear my phone."

Bill's face was unreadable, but his tone cut through the fog like a cold knife. "What's wrong with you?"

"Um, nothing," Simon lied, his voice a hollow echo of itself. "I'm tired, that's all."

Bill crossed his arms, his eyes narrowing in disbelief. "I can't have you around machinery like this, man. It's not safe. I'm sorry, you gotta go."

Simon's heart sank, though it didn't fully register. Everything felt distant, as though he was watching his life unravel from outside of himself. "It's okay. I'm fine," he tried, his voice lacking conviction.

Bill shook his head, exasperated. "No, you're not. Last week, you rolled into the bread pallets. We can't be sending out busted-ass loaves of bread. How are people supposed to make their toast? Slices won't fit in the slot thingies." He paused, sighing deeply. "I gotta un-hire you, Simon. No more chances."

Simon felt the words hit him, but they didn't sink in, not completely. His body was numb, his mind too cloudy to process what was happening. He'd failed again, and it was nothing new.

"Fine," Simon mumbled, barely audible. "I'll go."

He tried to back up the golf cart, but Bill was already stepping forward, waving his hands. "Simon! Stop. Stop. You can't drive this anymore. Just... walk out. Walk, man."

"The cart's the best part," Simon replied, almost childlike in his protest.

Bill handed Simon his hard hat, tool belt, walkie-talkie, and truck keys. His voice was a bit cautious, as if talking to a wounded animal. "You keep these. But don't drive home just yet, okay?"

Simon shook his head. "I told you, I'm tired."

Bill's expression tightened, sympathy flickering in his eyes. "Yeah. Get better, man."

Simon turned away, the reality of his firing barely registering in the haze. His body moved on autopilot, his feet dragging as he walked away with his head down, failure hanging over him like a dark cloud. He felt small, like a sad little kid who had just been scolded.

He knew Angie would be furious. How could he tell her that he'd screwed up again, that he'd lost another job because of his addiction? The drugs had numbed the immediate sting of regret, but beneath it all, he knew. He was losing everything. Slowly. Irrevocably.

As Simon trudged away from the warehouse, the world around him seemed quieter, emptier. Each step was a reminder of the distance between him and the life he once thought he could salvage.

With no plan, no purpose, and no way to fix the mess he'd made, Simon walked into the night, a ghost of the man he once was.

Thirty-Five

Faith, Love, and Never Say Die

Angie sought a bit of relief, a break from the whirlwind that had become her life with Simon. A separation wasn't going to happen, but a breather was needed. The constant battle with his addiction, the endless cycle of hope and despair, had left her drained. So, when her sister Rosie invited her out to Texas for a visit, Angie seized the opportunity. It wasn't running away, she told herself. Just a chance to clear her head, to get some distance and perspective.

The white pick-up truck cruised along the smooth asphalt road, a small crucifix swaying from the rearview mirror with each turn. The warm Texas air poured in through the open windows, whipping through Angie's hair as she gazed out at the passing scenery. Beside her, Rosie gripped the steering wheel, her eyes focused on the road ahead as Fort Hood's entrance loomed into view.

"This shouldn't take too long," Rosie said, glancing at her sister with a slight grin. "I just gotta drop off some paperwork. Unless you wanna stop at the PX?"

Angie's lips curled into a tired smile. "Tax free, hella yes. That's the only reason to visit you."

Rosie laughed, and the sound was a brief balm to the tension that had been building in the air between them. "Last week, they had some really pretty wind chimes. I think I'll get one for Mom."

They passed through the gates of the base, the imposing structures giving way to neat rows of buildings and the quiet order of military life. As they drove, a small chapel came into view, standing humbly among the surrounding buildings. Angie's eyes lingered on it, her mind elsewhere, as though the sight of it stirred something deep inside her.

"What's that?" Angie asked suddenly.

Rosie blinked, glancing at the chapel before returning her eyes to the road. "It's the chapel," she said matter-of-factly, her tone lacking the same reverence Angie felt.

"Can you stop, please?" Angie asked.

Rosie hesitated, eyebrows raised in surprise. "Um, ok. Why? There's no Mass right now, we're going tomorrow morning."

"Doesn't matter," Angie replied, her voice firm but distant. "I need to make a visit. Like Mom says. I haven't done that in a while."

Rosie pulled the truck to a stop, parking near the chapel entrance. She gave her sister a sidelong glance, skepticism and concern blending into her expression. "Like prayer is gonna cure him."

Angie exhaled sharply, tired of the criticism, tired of the disbelief. "No," she said, stepping out of the truck. "It's for me, I need it. I could use a little quiet. Why can't you just be supportive of my 'bad decision'? Who's it hurting? Me. Not you."

Both sisters exited the truck, the crunch of their footsteps on gravel filling the space between them as they walked toward the chapel.

"No. It hurts us to see you deal with that shit," Rosie said, her tone hard but not unfeeling. "You should hear Tony. He wants to kick his ass."

Angie stopped in her tracks, her eyes narrowing as she turned to face her sister. "Why? I'm choosing to stay with him."

Rosie's response came quick, sharp. "Waste of time! I don't know why you stay if you're miserable."

Angie's frustration boiled over. "You're right," she snapped, her voice breaking. "I am fucking miserable and tired and worried and crying all the time. How is that different from anyone else's life?"

Rosie blinked, caught off guard by the raw emotion in Angie's voice. "Um, normally people don't feel those things all at the same time without like a break in between," she said cautiously, her words meant to be light but missing the mark.

"Will you shut up?" Angie growled, resuming her pace toward the chapel, her fists clenched at her sides.

Rosie sighed, following closely behind. "Like you can't find someone who's not all screwed up."

"You don't get it," Angie said, her voice quieter now, more vulnerable. "You've always had your pick."

"Yeah, it's called not settling."

Angie stopped again, her eyes locking onto Rosie's, a quiet storm brewing beneath the surface. "Well, I'm the chick who got stood up by the first guy who asked her out on her first freakin' date."

Rosie's eyes widened in surprise and laughed. "What? I didn't know that."

"Only Mom knew," Angie said, her voice cracking. "It was humiliating."

"So Simon's the first..." Rosie began, her voice trailing off.

"Everything," Angie said simply, nodding as if that one word carried a thousand confessions. "Like I've told you."

Rosie shook her head, still not fully understanding. "So you settled for the first guy who touched you?"

"No!" Angie's voice was fierce, her eyes flashing with anger. "There's been no settling. I waited for someone who showed a genuine interest. Someone who actually wanted to know me."

"I don't totally get it," Rosie admitted, her voice less judgmental.

Angie let out a frustrated groan. "It's a connection thing, and I just love him. I'm not giving up, okay?"

Rosie rolled her eyes, her tone cynical. "You're so Lifetime. There's gotta be more to it. Is it the sex? 'Cause you never had it before? Never mind, don't want to know. But it's gotta be more than love."

Angie stopped walking, turning fully to face her sister. "Why?" she demanded. "Why does it have to be more? Maybe that's enough for stupid me. Maybe I'm the only one who can see that beyond the drugs, he's absolutely beautiful, and he loves me." A quiet sadness settled over her. "Look at Mom and Dad. They still love each other. So what if they had fought harder for that?"

Rosie shook her head, a bitter laugh escaping her lips. "Ugh, that's so movie of the week. So it's like 'Goonies never say die' kind of thing?"

Angie let out a small, defeated laugh. "Dork. But yes, exactly."

"But it feels like the 'cliffs of insanity,'" Angie added, a small smirk playing at the corners of her lips.

Rosie rolled her eyes but smiled. "Oh my gosh, you're so '80s."

Angie's smile widened. "We're so watching *The Princess Bride* tonight!"

"Or *Goonies*?" Rosie offered.

They both answered at the same time. "Princess Bride!"

Angie giggled, feeling the tension between them melt away, at least for now.

"And for the record," she added, casting a teasing glance at her sister. "The sex is amazing."

Rosie wrinkled her nose in mock disgust. "Gross."

As they walked toward the chapel doors, Angie felt a flicker of hope amidst the chaos in her life. Maybe it wasn't much, but it was enough to keep her going. Enough to fight for Simon. Enough to fight for herself. And for now, that was all she needed.

Thirty-Six

No Questions Asked

The waiting room was as outdated as the medical care Simon had come to expect. An anti-smoking poster from the '90s hung limply on the exam room wall. Simon sat slouched in the plastic chair, staring at the worn floor tiles, trying to ignore the dull ache radiating from his lower back. The discomfort was always there, simmering beneath the surface, but lately, it had flared up, consuming his thoughts and wearing him down.

He tried to shift in his seat, wincing as a sharp spasm shot through his muscles. His fingers grazed over the bulge in his pocket, the wad of cash, his ticket to relief. The money was both comforting and suffocating. This wasn't just about the pain anymore. It hadn't been for a long time.

The door creaked open, and in walked Dr. Kaczmarek but everyone called him, Dr. K. He was round in shape, balding, and with the kind of demeanor that seemed half-present. He shuffled through Simon's patient file, not making much eye contact.

“Mr. Wagner, good afternoon,” Dr. K said, a forced smile tugging at the corners of his lips.

"Hey, doc," Simon responded, trying to sound casual, but his voice sounded low, a gravelly rasp laced with exhaustion.

Dr. K sat down, glancing at the pain chart on the wall, the one with the smiley-to-sad faces. He pointed lazily at it. "So, what's hurting you today?"

Simon sighed, running a hand through his disheveled hair. "My lower back. It’s been killing me. Hurts when I pick something up, I can’t sleep. I feel anxious all the time. And these spasms, they’re bad."

Dr. K didn’t seem moved by the description, his eyes barely flickering from the chart. "On a scale of one to ten, what’s your pain level right now?"

Simon hesitated. The truth was, he wasn’t sure if the pain was still physical or if it had become something else, something deeper. "Probably an eight," he said, settling on a number that sounded bad enough to justify what he was about to do.

Dr. K leaned back in his chair, studying Simon in that detached way he always did. "And how can I help you with this?"

This was routine. Simon didn’t need to explain. He reached into his pocket and pulled out the cash, placing it quietly on the stool between them.

Dr. K nodded, turning to count the money. Five hundred dollars. That was the price for today’s peace. He scribbled out prescriptions, his hand moving quickly across the pad, almost mechanically.

"Oxycodone," Dr. K murmured, looking up briefly for Simon’s approval. "Thirty milligrams. Somas for the muscle spasms, Xanax for the anxiety, and Valium to help you sleep. Did I miss anything?"

Simon shook his head. "No, doc. That'll help."

"I'm sure it will," Dr. K replied, the transaction complete. There was no warmth, no concern, just business. Just relief in a bottle.

Thirty-Seven

Lonely Hearts

The sunlight poured through the kitchen windows, illuminating the simple breakfast table where Susan and Hank sat together. Hank, engrossed in the Harbor Freight ad, sipped his coffee, flipping through the pages of tools and car parts. Susan, on the other hand, sat quietly, her hands cupped around a teacup, her eyes fixed on the wall as if it held some secret answer she was waiting to discover.

"That wall's not gonna change colors, you know," Hank muttered, not even looking up from the ad.

Susan didn't respond right away, her fingers absently tracing the rim of her cup. "Do you think it's odd that Simon hasn't called us?" she asked, her voice barely above a whisper.

Hank glanced up, a sigh escaping him. "I'm sure he's okay."

"But don't you want to know if he is?" Susan pressed, her concern etched in every word. There was an ache in her chest, the kind that only a mother could feel.

"I'm hoping he is," Hank replied, trying to sound more confident than he felt. "Either way, we don't have control over it."

Susan's gaze remained fixed on the wall, but her thoughts were with her son. "I miss him," she said, the words carrying years of worry and maternal instinct.

"You miss monitoring him," Hank corrected gently, though there was no malice in his tone. He understood Susan's pain, even if he couldn't let it consume him the way it did her.

"I miss my son, Hank," she said, more firmly this time. The son who used to help her with groceries, who had a laugh that filled the room, who hadn't yet been taken by addiction. She missed the boy who used to bring light into their home.

Hank lowered his ad, looking at Susan with a mixture of empathy and frustration. "I miss my son being sober. I miss the guy I could build cars with or go surfing with. That's what I miss."

"That's what I mean," Susan murmured, her voice trembling. "I miss him."

"But we can't enable him, Sus," Hank reminded her gently. His voice was steady, but his heart ached. "I can't even think about the worst that could happen... I can't. He'll come back when he's better."

The silence of unspoken fears. "I hope so," she whispered, tears stinging at the corners of her eyes.

Hank nodded, his hand reaching across the table to join hers. "Me too." His grip was firm, grounding them both in the moment, but a sadness lingered in his eyes. They both knew they were waiting for a day that might never come.

Thirty-Eight

Fading Lines

The sun was a dull haze in the afternoon sky, hanging low as Simon's truck rolled through the quiet park. The engine rumbled beneath him, a constant vibration that mirrored the inside of his own body, a restless energy, the kind that never seemed to go away. He spotted Johnny sitting on a weathered bench, cigarette dangling between his fingers, smoke curling up in lazy swirls. It was a scene they'd played out too many times before, like clockwork.

Simon eased the truck to a stop, gravel crunching under the tires, and Johnny, with his usual nonchalance, sauntered over and slipped into the passenger seat. The truck door creaked as it closed, sealing them in.

"What up, Scrill?" Johnny greeted, his voice tinged with excitement, he knew his fix was just moments away.

Simon offered a half-hearted nod, eyes already glazing over as the familiar script began to play out. "What up, playa'."

Johnny shifted in the seat, impatience lacing his next words. "Did you score some beans?"

Simon reached under the seat, pulling out a small plastic bag. It was second nature, the feel of the plastic, the weight of it in his hand. "You know it. Got some Oxy's, bars, Somas, and a few, uh, sleepers."

Johnny's eyes lit up as he handed over a crumpled wad of bills, counting them quickly before shoving them into Simon's palm. "Nice, man. Here, I got one seventy. I'll take a sampler."

But Simon, instead of just completing the exchange, hesitated for a moment. He handed over the pills but kept his eyes on the dashboard. "You tired of this, Johnny? You don't even need this shit."

Johnny blinked, taken aback. It wasn't like Simon to ask questions, to *care*. But Johnny brushed it off with a casual shrug. "But I like it. Look at you, man. You don't need it either."

The words stung, but Simon pushed the feeling down deep. He didn't want to feel anything right now. He needed the pills to numb that constant ache, the one that was more than just the physical pain from his accident. "Yeah, I do."

Johnny gave him a sideways glance, shaking his head like Simon was a puzzle he couldn't figure out. "But come on, you're not like in *super real* pain."

Simon didn't respond this time. He just shook his head, because how could Johnny understand? How could anyone understand the kind of pain that lived inside him, gnawing at his insides day after day? It wasn't just about his body anymore, it was his mind, his soul. The pills kept it all at bay, even if just for a little while.

Money exchanged hands, and Johnny stuffed the pills into his pocket, oblivious to the storm brewing inside his friend, grinned as he flicked his cigarette butt out the window and climbed out of the truck.

"Later, Scrill."

Simon barely nodded, watching Johnny disappear back toward the bench. He felt... empty. Like everything in his life had become a hollow routine, a series of motions he went through without meaning. His hand tightened on the steering wheel, but even that felt distant. Like it wasn't really his anymore.

Thirty-Nine

No Take Backs

Angie stood at the curb of the airport terminal. The retreat with her sister was over too soon. Her bag rested by her feet, one hand gripping her phone as the other hung by her side, fingers drumming restlessly against her thigh. The rhythmic pulse of traffic moved around her: cars pulling up to the airport terminal, people hopping in and out with luggage, and families reuniting in quick embraces. But for Angie, the waiting stretched past a test of patience into growing frustration. The minutes dragged on, each one longer than the last. Everything faded into the background as her focus stayed locked on the phone screen, willing it to light up with Simon's name.

The knot in her stomach tightened, a familiar mix of anxiousness twisting inside her. She glanced up and down the curb for what felt like the hundredth time, scanning for any sign of his truck. Still nothing.

With an irritated sigh, Angie tapped Simon's name on her contact list again. Her foot tapped nervously on the concrete as the phone rang and rang before finally going to voicemail.

"Hey, it's Si, tell me why," came his lazy, almost indifferent greeting on the recorded message.

She hung up, her hand trembling slightly as she stared at the phone in disbelief. *What the hell, Simon?* Her mind racing as she dialed him again, this time her jaw clenched tighter. The call rang through, and finally, he picked up.

"Hey," Simon's voice thick, slow, like he was dragging every syllable through molasses.

"Finally," Angie snapped, her relief at hearing his voice quickly replaced by anger. "Where are you?"

On the other end, Simon blinked, struggling to stay focused as the world outside his windshield blurred into one long stretch of highway. The steering wheel under his hands, the truck's vibrations sending him into a dangerous half-sleep. He wasn't fully aware of where he was, the edges of his mind clouded by whatever combination of pills he had taken earlier.

"I'm on my way to pick you up," he mumbled, trying to sound casual, though his words slurred together.

Angie rolled her eyes, trying to keep her temper in check. "I figured that. How far away are you?"

Simon blinked again, his vision hazy. The truck drifted slightly to the right, tires brushing the shoulder of the road. He glanced out the window, struggling to find his bearings. "Oh, you know... by some water," he said vaguely, as if that answer made sense.

Angie's brows furrowed, her grip tightening on the phone. "Simon? What are you talking about? Where are you now?"

There was static on the line, the connection crackling. Angie could hear the distant roar of wind coming through his end, but his voice was fading. "You're breaking up," she called, her heart beginning to race. The dread that had been gnawing at her all day suddenly sharpened, becoming something more immediate, more urgent.

The call dropped, leaving Angie staring at her phone, her heart pounding. She hit redial, the ringing seeming louder in her ears now, but there was no answer. She tried again, nothing.

"Shit," she muttered under her breath. She could feel her pulse in her throat, her mind spinning in circles of worry. Something wasn't right.

Simon barely registered the phone slipping from the seat onto the floor, his head too foggy to react. His eyes were half-closed, fighting the pull of sleep washing over him in waves. The pills were hitting harder than he expected, to the point where everything outside the truck felt like a dream, far away, unreal.

The highway stretched ahead of him. His body felt disconnected from his mind, his hands clumsy on the steering wheel.

"Hey, Ang," he muttered to no one, his voice thick with the haze of the high. "I'm trying to drive... we'll talk later." He wasn't even sure if she was still on the line.

Angie stood at the curb, pacing now, her phone still clutched in her hand. She was clenching her jaw, a nervous habit she'd picked up over the years whenever things with Simon were spiraling out of control. She kept looking up and down the terminal, hoping to see his truck come into view, but with each passing minute, the worry gnawed at her harder.

Finally, after what felt like an eternity, Simon's truck pulled up to the curb. The way he braked, the rough, jerky stop, immediately set off alarms in Angie's mind. Her stomach dropped as she grabbed her bag and threw it into the back, climbing into the passenger seat without a word.

"You're an hour and a half late," she said sharply, not bothering to hide her irritation.

Simon turned to her with a slow, lazy grin, his eyes half-lidded as if he didn't even register her anger. "Hi, beautiful," he slurred, reaching over as if to take her hand.

But Angie pulled away, too upset to notice how his words barely made sense, too upset to realize she should be driving. The silence in the truck was deafening as they drove, neither of them speaking.

Simon gripped the steering wheel with trembling hands, trying to focus on the road, but the words kept swimming around in his head. *I'm trying, Ang... I'm trying.*

But even he knew it wasn't enough.

The sun draped the Pacific Coast Highway in a warm, serene glow. The waves crashing against the rocky cliffs below whispered of calm. Angie leaned against the window, the sound of the ocean lulling her into a light, uneasy doze. The warmth of the sunset bathed her face, momentarily easing the turmoil churning inside her.

Simon's hands gripped the steering wheel, but his mind was elsewhere. His eyes drooped lower with each passing mile, the road ahead becoming a blur of asphalt and fading light. The pills had dulled his senses, the high that once made him feel invincible now betraying him in the most dangerous way. His head nodded, his grip on consciousness slipping further with each second.

The truck began to drift, first slowly, then more noticeably as it crossed onto the shoulder, the rough rumble of the tires over gravel jolting the truck.

Angie stirred, her senses snapping back to alertness as the unfamiliar roughness under the tires rattled her awake. Her heart spiked as she turned, seeing Simon's head hanging low, his eyes barely open.

"Simon!" she yelled, slapping his arm hard.

The truck jerked violently as Simon, startled awake, yanked the steering wheel in a desperate overcorrection. The truck swerved sharply across the highway, the tires screeching as they struggled to regain traction. The world outside the windows blurred, and before Angie could process what was happening, a blinding crash echoed through the truck. The sound of metal grinding against metal filled the air, followed by the violent impact of the truck sideswiping another car.

The world spun.

Angie's breath caught in her throat as the truck twirled out of control, her hands gripping the seat as the centrifugal force pressed her against the door. The screeching sound of tires, the sickening crunch of metal, and the sheer chaos of motion overwhelmed her senses. Her heart pounded in her chest, every muscle tensing as she braced for the unknown.

The truck finally skidded to a stop, the violent momentum throwing it toward the edge of the cliffside. Dust and dirt filled the air, clouding the world around her in a suffocating haze. Angie's ears rang with the sound of the crash, her entire body shaking from the shock. She blinked rapidly, her vision blurred as adrenaline surged through her veins.

For a moment, everything was silent. The dust settled in the fading light of the sunset, casting an eerie stillness over the wreckage. Angie took a shallow breath, her chest tight as she looked down at her hands, at her body. She seemed unharmed, the seatbelt having done its job, but the trembling in her limbs betrayed the terror racing through her.

Her eyes darted to Simon, panic surging inside her again as she reached for him. "Simon!" Her voice was hoarse, barely more than a whisper as she shook him, her heart pounding. "Simon, are you okay?"

He didn't respond at first, his head lolling to the side, his eyes half-closed. Angie's hands trembled as she slapped his cheek gently, her breath catching in her throat.

He mumbled something incoherent, his words slurred, his eyes struggling to focus on her.

Relief and frustration warred inside her, a sob catching in her throat.

The sun was setting, the warm hues of sunset replaced by the cold, artificial glow of police lights and ambulance sirens. The once serene highway had transformed into a scene of chaos. Police officers, paramedics, and tow trucks filled the area, working to clear the wreckage.

Angie stood by the tow truck, her arms wrapped tightly around herself as she watched the scene unfold. Her breath came in shallow bursts, her mind reeling from everything that had happened in the past hour. Her hands were still shaking, her eyes stinging from unshed tears.

She watched as paramedics loaded the other driver onto a stretcher. Angie felt a pang of guilt deep in her chest. Someone else had been hurt because of this mess they were trapped in.

Her gaze shifted to Simon. He was failing the sobriety test miserably, his movements uncoordinated, his eyes unfocused. The officer holding the breathalyzer shook his head, a look of disappointment and resignation on his face.

Simon stumbled, mumbling something Angie couldn't hear, his hands shaky as the officer grabbed him by the arm. And then, with a swift and practiced motion, the officer clicked the handcuffs around Simon's wrists. The metal clanged in the night air. It was like watching a slow-motion version of her worst fears play out in front of her.

Angie's heart shattered as she saw Simon being led toward the squad car. His head hung low, his steps unsteady as if he was barely aware of what was happening. The pills, the addiction, the lies. The familiar wave of emotional overwhelm crashed down upon her.

From where she stood by the tow truck, Angie felt like she was watching it all from a distance, a spectator in the disintegration of her life. Tears blurred her vision, but she didn't move. She couldn't.

FORTY

FRAYED AND CONFUSED

Angie opened the door to the apartment, immediately overwhelmed by the sheer chaos that greeted her. The clutter felt like a physical presence, crowding the small space, suffocating her. Papers were strewn across the floor, mingled with socks, hats, and random bits of hiking gear. Books were haphazardly stacked, some on the floor, others teetering on the edge of the coffee table. The place was a mess, a reflection of the whirlwind her life had become.

Her eyes landed on a bag of SunChips clipped to the blinds with a clothespin. She let out a small, nervous laugh at the absurdity of it. *I was only gone for four days!* It wasn't just the mess; it was everything. The wreckage of their relationship, the addiction that had stolen Simon from her bit by bit. The SunChips dangling like a bizarre flag in the corner was just one more thing in a long list of things she couldn't control.

Exhausted, she shuffled through the mess and collapsed onto the bed, too tired to even change. Fully clothed, she grabbed her cell phone, holding it tightly in her hand as if it were a lifeline. The reality of it all hung over her like a dark cloud. *He's in jail.*

Simon leaned against the cold steel of the holding cell, his body coming down from the high, his head pounding with the dull ache of regret. The buzz that had dulled his pain earlier now left him hollow, empty. He stared blankly at the floor as the officers processed him, moving him along the assembly line of booking: fingerprints, mugshot, paperwork. His mind felt as chaotic as the room Angie had walked into, like pieces scattered everywhere, impossible to put back together.

The fluorescent lights flickered overhead, casting a harsh glare on his reality. Everything had blurred, each bad decision bleeding into the next until he couldn't see where one ended and the other began. His mind flashed to the crash, to Angie's voice screaming his name, the terror in her eyes. I could've killed her.

The officer's voice broke through his haze. "You get one call."

Simon's mouth was dry, as he was led to the bank of phones. He stood there for a moment, staring at the receiver as if it held all the answers he didn't have. He picked it up, dialing the number he knew by heart, hoping she would answer.

The apartment was silent. Angie couldn't fight the exhaustion, her mind too tired to keep running through an endless loop. She wasn't sure how to feel, was she relieved that Simon was in jail, that maybe, this would be the rock bottom he needed to get help? Was there a rock bottom? Or was she just too numb to feel anything at all?

The house phone on the nightstand rang, the sudden noise jarring her awake. She blinked groggily, momentarily disoriented before realizing what it was. The landline. It rang again.

She scrambled to pick it up, her heart already pounding in her chest.

"Hello?" Her voice came out raspy, thick with sleep.

An automated voice cut through the line. "This is a collect call from the Ventura County Sheriff Department of Corrections calling on behalf of..." Simon's voice, hollow and distant, echoed through the automated system. "Simon Wagner," Will you accept the charges?"

Angie's throat tightened. "Yes, yes," she said quickly, her hands shaking.

There was a pause, and then his voice. "Hey," Simon said, his tone quiet.

"Hey," Angie responded, her voice a mix of exhaustion and wariness.

"Are you okay?" he asked, the question loaded with guilt.

Angie let out a bitter laugh, shaking her head even though he couldn't see her. "I don't know."

"I'm sorry," Simon mumbled, the words almost inaudible.

Her frustration flared. "Do you know what happened, Simon?

"We crashed," he stated simply.

"You passed out and crashed the truck! With us in it! While it was moving!," Angie's voice was more exhausted than angry, she didn't want to fight, she wanted to forget.

There was a long pause. "Yeah," he finally said, his voice thick with regret. "I know."

"You could've..." Angie's voice cracked. "You could've killed us, Simon. You could've killed someone else."

"I know," Simon's voice was barely a whisper, the shame evident.

"I should've been driving, I was so mad you were late I didn't even think about it. But where does it stop?" Angie's voice trembled with both anger and sadness. "When does this end?"

A deep, suffocating silence hung between them. Both fought back tears, neither willing to let the dam break.

A sharp beep cut through the line, signaling that their time was almost up.

"So... what happens now?" Angie asked, the anger dissipating into sheer exhaustion.

"I guess they'll keep me here until tomorrow morning. Then I'm out."

Angie closed her eyes, fighting the overwhelming sense of helplessness. "Well, I guess I'll come pick you up tomorrow," she said, her voice barely above a whisper.

"You don't have to."

"Who else is there?" she replied, the question hanging between them, filled with all the things left unsaid.

The line clicked, and then went dead.

Forty-One

Too Late for Second Thoughts

Angie sat in the stillness of the apartment, Simon's collect call on her mind. Her body felt drained, as if all the life had been sapped out of her. She rubbed her temples, trying to ease the tension, but the ache wasn't just physical. It was deeper, a gnawing, hollow pain in her chest. Her thoughts drifted, pulling her away from the chaos and mess around her.

The late afternoon sun bathed the hilltop. Angie and Simon were seated on a wooden bench, perched on the crest of the Two Trees hill, a local hiking spot they'd come to love. The air was crisp, the breeze gentle, carrying the scent of the sea and wildflowers. Below them, the city sprawled out in quiet simplicity, but up here, they were in their own world.

The remnants of their picnic were scattered between them; an empty wine bottle, a few crumbs from the sandwiches they'd devoured, and a half-eaten apple Angie had been absentmindedly picking at.

Angie glanced over at Simon, smiling to herself. His eyes were fixed on the view, but there was a seriousness about him, a quiet thoughtfulness.

"Angie," Simon started, his voice breaking through the tranquil silence. "I've been thinking."

She looked up, her curiosity piqued. "Uh oh, that's always dangerous."

Simon smirked, shaking his head. "Nah, this is serious. I think..." He paused, searching her face. "I think we should get married."

Angie's heart skipped a beat, her body freezing as if the air had suddenly become still. A nervous chuckle escaped her lips. "What?" She blinked at him, unsure if she'd heard correctly.

"I'm serious," Simon repeated, his eyes sincere. "I think we should get married."

Her breath caught in her throat, emotions swirling around her like the gentle wind. She studied his face for a moment, trying to process what he'd said. "Are you asking me?" There was a lightness in her voice, a teasing lilt that masked the rush of emotions suddenly flooding her.

"Not yet," Simon said, shaking his head slightly. "I want to ask your dad first. You know, get his blessing and all."

Angie smiled, warmth spreading through her. "So... you just want to know if I like the idea?"

Simon nodded, his gaze held hers. "Yeah. Do you?"

The simplicity of his question, the way he'd asked it so casually, felt so perfectly Simon. He wasn't one for grand gestures. He was straightforward, honest, and real. And that's what she loved about him.

"Very much so," she replied, her voice quiet but full of certainty.

"Cool," Simon grinned, his boyish smile spreading across his face. "It's gonna be simple though, you know. I hope you're not expecting some big poem or me busting out a guitar solo."

Angie laughed, shaking her head. "No, that's definitely not our style." She nudged him playfully. "We're simple folk, remember?"

Simon leaned closer, his hand brushing against hers. "You're my girl, Angie. You know that, right? You've got my heart."

A rush of emotion swelled in her chest, the love she had for him overwhelming her in that moment. She didn't need anything more than this. Just him, just them, together. "Yeah, and you've got mine too," she whispered, feeling the truth of it settle into her bones.

"I love you, sugar," Simon said, his eyes never leaving hers.

A mischievous glint flickered in Angie's eyes as she leaned in. "Show me."

And with that, Simon pulled her into his arms, his lips pressing against hers in a kiss that was filled with promise, with love, with everything that was them. The sun dipped lower in the sky, casting long shadows across the hill, but up there, on that bench, they were wrapped in their own golden light.

The memory faded as Angie blinked herself back to the present, the clutter of the apartment reappearing in her vision. The mess around her, the emotional chaos of their current situation, contrasted so sharply with that peaceful moment on the hilltop.

Back then, it had all felt so easy. Their love had been strong, simple, untainted by the mess of pills, lies, and destruction. She could still feel the warmth of that day on her skin and a future together that had seemed so clear.

Angie stood up, moving through the apartment as if in a daze. The love between them wasn't enough to fix everything.

Forty-Two

The Storm After the Storm

The rain had just passed, leaving the streets wet and glistening in the early morning light. Angie sat in her car, staring out of the foggy windshield, waiting for Simon to walk out of the jailhouse. Her fingers absentmindedly picked at the steering wheel, tapping it with a quiet, nervous rhythm. Each tap echoed the tension in her chest, a knot tightening with every passing second. She exhaled a shaky breath, trying to gather herself, but everything felt unbearable.

Outside, a handful of men trickled out of the building, Simon among them. He was bumming a cigarette off the guy next to him, lighting up with a practiced ease that made Angie's stomach churn. When he spotted her, his eyes flickered with a brief, dull recognition. He flicked the cigarette away and started walking toward the car, the casualness of his movements like a slap to her face.

Simon slid into the passenger seat, the door creaking shut behind him. The silence that followed was thick, suffocating.

"Hey," he muttered, his voice void of any real emotion.

Angie gripped the steering wheel tighter, her knuckles turning white. *That's it?* she thought. *Just hey?*

"Hi," she responded, her voice hollow.

For a moment, they just sat there. Angie's chest felt like it was going to explode. She had waited, *hoped*, for something more from him. Something that would make sense of everything, some sign that he was genuinely sorry, that he understood the gravity of what had happened. But all she got was, "Hey."

As the silence stretched, her frustration bubbled over. Her foot pressed down harder on the gas, hands gripping the wheel as if it were the only thing holding her together.

"That's it?" she snapped, the words tumbling out before she could stop them. "Just *hey*?"

Simon didn't meet her gaze. He leaned back in the seat, letting out a long breath. "What do you want me to say?" he muttered. "I said sorry."

Angie's eyes flashed with fury, the anger surging up like a tidal wave. She couldn't believe him. Couldn't believe how unaffected he seemed. "You almost *fucking killed us*!" she shouted, her voice rising with each word. "I'm waiting for some kind of goddamned enlightenment! Something, anything!"

She glanced at him, searching his face for a reaction, but all she saw was indifference. Simon shrugged, his voice flat. "I just got busted for a DUI. I'm sorry I'm not all hippie-dippie crystal clear over here."

Angie's heart pounded in her chest, each beat loud and painful. Her world was crumbling around her, and Simon... Simon was *this*. "Yesterday was one of the worst days of my life, Simon," she said, her voice breaking. "My life, our shitty life, flashed before me. And I looked at you, and there was nothing. *Where's my Simon?* Where's the man who made me feel like I was home? Now I'm here with my puffy cry eyes and the worst headache I've ever had, thank you, and you just say "hey."

Her words hung in the air, but Simon had no answer. He stared out the window, detached, as if this wasn't happening to him too.

Angie couldn't take it anymore. She yanked the car into a parking lot and pulled to a stop at a city park. Without a word, she threw open the door, stormed out, and slammed it shut. The frustration, the exhaustion. She spotted a puddle and stomped in it, sending water splashing up her legs. But it wasn't enough. Bystanders on the nearby path quickly got out of her way. She stomped harder, searching for another, bigger puddle. One that would make her feel better.

From the car, Simon watched her with a mixture of nervousness and confusion.

"And you don't seem fazed by it at all." Her rage continued, she ran back to the car, opened and slammed the door again. Then she ran over to a chain linked fence. Angie grabbed the fence and began to throw another tantrum. She rattled the fence, jumped up and down, flailing her arms all while just letting sounds out.

"Angie!" Simon calls to her, finally stepping out of the car and running over to her. "Hey! Hold on. Jesus, what the hell kind of crazy is this?"

She turned back toward him, her voice raw and out of breath, "I don't know. I'm just tired, I'm frustrated, I'm scared. I can't...I can't..."

Simon's brow furrowed. He didn't know what to say. What *could* he say?

She continues, "Do something! Say something! *Show me something!*" Angie is spent. She turns her back to the fence and slides down, her butt hitting the wet grass. "Just TALK to me!"

For a moment, Simon was silent, his mind racing but blank at the same time. What could he say? What could he possibly say to make this better? "I'm scared too," he admitted. "Right now, all I'm thinking about is how to get more pills so I don't go into withdrawals. I feel like shit, Ang. I feel like I'm drying up."

Angie's eyes were wide, her breaths coming faster. "That's it?" she demanded. "That's all you have to say? Nothing about yesterday? Nothing about what you almost did?"

"It doesn't work like that," Simon muttered. "I know I fucked up. I know I'm fucked up."

Her heart pounded harder, the tears she'd been holding back finally spilling over. "Do you need a more dramatic rock bottom?!" she cried. "Is that it? How does this play out, Simon? Do you die in a ditch? Do you kill someone in another crash and get sober in prison? Or do you OD, and I'm the one who finds you cold with foam and shit coming out of your mouth?"

Simon's face paled. "You can't help me, Ang."

"Which is it, Simon?" she pressed. "Pick one."

"What?" He shook his head, confused.

"Choose," she repeated, her voice hard.

Simon answered matter of factly. "OD."

Angie let out a bitter, broken laugh. "Fan-fucking-tastic. So, you leave on a high note, and I get to find your body. I get to live with *that* for the rest of my life. Thanks, Simon."

"Let's just... leave it all here," Simon said quietly, his voice cracking. "Clean break. You walk away, 'cause there's no quick fix here. This shit's gonna drag on. I told you, you could do better."

"No," Angie shot back, her voice fierce. "You don't get to give up on us. That's mine, not yours. I decide when I'm done with all this shit.. *Got it?*"

Simon stood there, speechless.

"Do you want to be better than this?" Angie asked, her voice suddenly calm but firm. "It's a yes or no question. Yes or no, Simon."

Simon hesitated, then nodded. "Yes."

"Then start." Angie got up, beginning to walk away, the exhaustion in her body palpable. She didn't head back to the car; she needed to walk, to breathe, to think.

Behind her, Simon stood there, lost. "It's not easy, Angie."

"It's not supposed to be, Simon," she said without looking back. "You decide the where, when and how of it. Figure out how you get better and fight for that."

As she walked away, Simon watched her, his heart aching in a way he hadn't expected. "I'm terrified, Ang".

She turned toward him, "Ok."

Simon hesitated. "I don't know who I am anymore," he admitted, his voice trembling. "That's the first clear thought I've had in... in a long time."

"Good," Angie encouraged, her voice still thick with emotion. "Keep going."

Simon ran a hand through his hair, his eyes staring at the ground. "I have to rebuild me. Like... inside out, head to toe. I need to learn how to cope with life, with pain, with everything that comes with it. I know I've been hiding from it all, but I need to face it. I know that."

Angie shook her head, her voice firm. "I don't need to hear it, Simon. I don't care how deep you search or what mountain you've gotta fucking climb." Her eyes locked onto his. "Honey, hop on that horse and ride like the wind. Just show yourself...stop following me."

Simon took a shaky breath. "Can you take me home?"

"I need a walk," Angie said, shaking her head. "I need to clear my head."

"You're walking home?" Simon asked, confused. "But the car..."

"Don't care," Angie replied flatly, already starting to walk away from him.

Simon stood there, rooted to the spot. He turned in the opposite direction for a moment, but something pulled him back. He followed her from a distance, unsure if she even wanted him near, but too afraid to let her walk away completely.

Forty-Three

Upside Is Down

The smell of old wood floors and plaster walls filled the small hall at St. Francis Church. It was a quiet, safe space, where whispered prayers mixed with the occasional clatter of coffee cups from the refreshments table. Angie sat next to Benjamin, her hands resting in her lap, trying to gather her thoughts. She'd been to this support group a few times now, but each visit felt different, sometimes comforting, sometimes suffocating, but always necessary.

Fr. Charles, dressed in one of his signature Hawaiian shirts, stood at the front, his presence somehow making the room feel lighter despite the heavy conversations that often took place here. Tonight's shirt was a riot of bright colors; red, green, and yellow flowers swirling across his torso. It made him feel approachable as if his churchly authority was held in suspense for a short while. Here, he was just like Angie.

Benjamin cleared his throat. His voice, though steady, held the tremor of vulnerability that came from opening up wounds not quite healed. "I prayed that my father would find peace before he died," he said, his eyes fixed on the far wall. "And I think he did. Forgiving him wasn't easy, but I think we both finally found it."

Angie glanced sideways at him, her heart squeezing with a mix of empathy and admiration. Benjamin had always carried his pain with quiet dignity, a strength she sometimes envied. His story wasn't too far from hers, yet it always felt like he had somehow navigated the minefield of addiction and recovery with a grace she couldn't quite find for herself.

"Thank you, Ben," Fr. Charles said, his voice gentle and filled with that peculiar mix of reverence and ease that he always carried. "Would anyone else like to share?"

The room fell silent for a moment, the kind of stillness that begged for release but was always hesitant to come. Angie felt her heart quicken, her thoughts jumbling into one another as she raised her hand.

"Hi," she began, her voice small but determined. "I'm Angie, and my husband is my addict." The words felt foreign, like they belonged to someone else, but they were hers. "He's been sober now for... just a few days, hours really. I've heard some of you talk about 'your person in recovery,' and I hope I can say that someday soon. But... right now... I'm starting to see *him* again. And that's great, but... it's strange. You spend so much time wanting them to stop using, and then they do... and now everything that should feel normal doesn't."

Her voice wavered. The vulnerability in her words felt like a thin thread holding her together, one tug away from unraveling completely. A tissue box was passed her way, the crinkle of tissues being pulled loud in the quiet of the room.

"It's like," Angie continued, "you want so much for them to stop and get clean, and when they finally do, you don't know how to act. You don't know how to feel about normal anymore. Why does normal feel so... complicated? Why can't I just enjoy the day being boring?"

Her words hung in the air, thick with the confusion she'd been carrying for weeks. She had spent so long living on the edge of chaos, always bracing for the next disaster. And now, with Simon nearing sobriety it felt like she had lost her footing, like she was falling into a different kind of uncertainty. The kind that whispered it could all come crashing down again any second.

Fr. Charles leaned forward, clasping his hands together as he spoke with the same ease he always did. "I think that's something that resonates with all of us here," he said, his gaze sweeping across the room. "The trust, the stability, the want for routine again, it all takes time to rebuild. Time and patience. We get used to chaos because it becomes our normal. But when that chaos is gone, we have to learn how to live again in the quiet. It's okay that it feels uncomfortable, that it feels like you're waiting for the other shoe to drop. It takes time. Just time."

His words lingered in the air, offering both comfort and truth that Angie wasn't sure she was ready to fully embrace. How long could she wait? How long before normal didn't feel like the calm before the next storm?

"Alright, break time folks!" Fr. Charles stood, clapping his hands together with a smile. "Mrs. Gutierrez baked her famous shortbread cookies, so make sure you grab one before they're gone."

The tension in the room eased as the members began to move, some heading toward the refreshments table, others simply sitting in quiet reflection. Angie let out a breath she didn't know she was holding. Benjamin placed a gentle hand on her shoulder, giving her a supportive squeeze before heading toward the cookies.

She stayed seated, though, her thoughts still swirling in the echo of her own voice. And yet, in her heart, she knew that boredom had never felt so far away. Even with Simon sober, it was as if the chaos still had a hold on her, like a shadow she couldn't shake. And as she sat there, staring blankly at the tissue in her hand, she wondered when, *if,* that would ever change.

FORTY-FOUR

HALFWAY TO SOMEWHERE

The apartment was dimly lit, a single lamp barely cutting through the stillness. Angie moved quietly around the small space. She had unfolded the futon earlier, pulling out blankets and a pillow in the hope of a few hours of sleep, though she knew it wouldn't come easily. The apartment was far too quiet, save for the occasional groan that slipped from Simon's throat as he tossed and turned in their bed behind the curtain.

The air felt suffocating with the tension that hung between them, between Simon and his body, and between Angie and the helplessness that gnawed at her insides. She heard him shift again, the muffled sound of his voice seeping through the thin fabric of the curtain that separated them. She paused, staring at the ceiling for a moment before finally getting up.

Moving behind the curtain, Angie found Simon buried beneath a pile of pillows, his body contorted as if he were trying to hide from the pain. His head was mostly covered, but even in the dim light, she could see the tension in his muscles, the way his feet dug into the mattress as if searching for some relief.

"Do you need anything else?" she asked, though the words felt hollow. She already knew the answer.

A muffled "No" came from beneath the pillows.

Angie crossed her arms, watching him for a moment, helplessness sinking in. "What does it feel like?" she asked, her voice quiet but persistent, wanting to understand what he was going through but knowing she couldn't truly comprehend.

Simon groaned, shifting slightly, his voice strained. "Weird. Like... I'm on my way down. I don't know, it's hard to explain. You know how when you get the flu, you feel like your body is foggy?"

"Yeah," she replied, nodding even though he couldn't see her.

"It's like that... I can feel it coming," he continued, his words slurring slightly from fatigue. "Like my body's about to collapse."

"Do you feel nauseous?" Angie asked, trying to keep the conversation going, though the concern in her voice was evident.

"Not right now," Simon answered, his tone flat. "The headache is the worst, and it's on its way."

Angie felt a surge of frustration and sadness. She couldn't do anything to make this easier for him. No matter how many times she checked on him, no matter how many blankets she brought or soothing words she whispered, it wouldn't change the fact that Simon was fighting a battle with his own body.

Later, Angie lay on the futon, her eyes staring into the darkened ceiling. She could hear Simon's breathing from behind the curtain, the occasional groan or restless movement breaking the silence. Each sound tugged at her heart, reminding her of his fragile state. Sleep wouldn't come tonight. How could it when the person she loved most was breaking down right in front of her?

Simon's moans grew louder, and Angie couldn't ignore them any longer. She threw the blankets aside and crossed the room to the bed. Behind the curtain, she found him curled up in a childlike pose, his body tangled in the sheets, pillow covering his head as if that could block out the pain. His feet dug into the mattress, his toes gripping at the sheets as though searching for a way out.

"You need anything?" Angie asked again, though she knew the answer hadn't changed.

Simon groaned, not bothering to lift his head. "No, just... sleep. I want nothing but sleep, but I can't because my head fucking hurts."

Angie sighed, leaning against the doorframe, helplessness threatening to choke her. "Is it getting worse?" she asked, her voice barely above a whisper.

"Uh-huh," Simon mumbled.

Angie nodded slowly, a bitter smile tugging at the corners of her mouth. "Good. That's progress." It was a cruel truth, but it was the truth. The worse it got, the closer he came to coming out the other side.

As another early morning crept in, Simon dragged himself out of bed, his body hunched over, defeated. He staggered to the bathroom, hovering over the toilet, his face pale and slick with sweat. He dry heaved, his body shaking with the effort, but nothing came. Exhausted, he stumbled back to bed, collapsing face-first into the pillows, his groans quieter now but no less painful.

By midday, the apartment was a cave of shadows. Before leaving for work, Angie had draped blankets over the windows, blocking out the daylight, hoping the darkness might soothe Simon's aching head. The house was eerily quiet except for the sound of running water from the bathroom. Simon stood in his underwear, leaning over the sink, rinsing his face. He stared into the mirror, his reflection looking back at him like a stranger. His eyes were sunken, his skin pale, but somewhere beneath the weariness, he thought maybe he looked a little better than shit.

A knock at the door broke the silence, startling him. He moved slowly, almost cautiously, and cracked the door open. Tony stood on the other side, a grin on his face, but the light that poured into the apartment was anything but welcome.

"What up, brother!" Tony's voice was loud, too loud for Simon's pounding head, and he winced as the sunlight hit him square in the face. Without waiting for an invitation, Tony walked in.

"Hey, man," Simon mumbled, still leaning against the doorframe for support.

Tony glanced around the dim apartment, taking in the mess and the staleness of the air. "What is this, day four or five?" Tony asked, clapping Simon on the back.

"I don't know," Simon muttered. "Something like that."

"Yeah, Angie told me," Tony said. "You hungry?"

Simon hesitated, unsure. "Yeah, kind of."

Tony gave him a grin and nodded toward the door. "Well, clean up, let's go."

Simon stared at him for a moment, caught between withdrawal and the fleeting hope that maybe things would get better.

"Yeah," he said quietly. "Okay."

Forty-Five

Figuring It Out (Sort Of)

The sun beat down hard on the small, bustling takeout window of *Coralie's*, the local spot for some of the best Mexican food in town. The line was long, a mix of construction workers, office employees, and locals on their lunch break, all waiting patiently for their burrito of choice. The scent of carne asada and warm tortillas filled the air, but for Simon, the smell didn't bring the usual comfort it once had.

He sat across from Tony at a small, wooden picnic table just outside the takeout window. The table wobbled slightly on the uneven pavement as they both unwrapped their burritos. Tony dove in immediately, savoring each bite as though he'd been deprived of good food for far too long.

"Mmm, mmm. So good," Tony mumbled through a mouthful of rice and beans, leaning back, clearly enjoying himself. "I missed my family, man, but the food... no place like Cali."

Simon barely looked up from his burrito. His appetite was nearly nonexistent, his stomach churning more from anxiety and everything that had happened than from hunger. He took a small bite, chewing mechanically, but it tasted like nothing.

“No doubt,” Simon muttered, eyes downcast as he wiped his mouth with a napkin. He dropped his burrito onto the wrapper.

Tony wasn’t deterred. He kept chewing and talking, trying to bridge the gap between them that felt wider than it should. “Now that I’m back stateside, we can kick it more, you know? Get the crew together. Just like old times."

“Yeah.” Simon’s response was flat, disinterested, and Tony caught the note of emptiness in his tone. The usual lightness between them felt strained, like a guitar string pulled too tight, on the verge of snapping.

Tony paused, burrito halfway to his mouth, and leaned forward. "You still talking to Johnny and those guys?"

Simon shook his head slowly, staring at the plate as if it held all the answers he couldn’t find. "I’m trying not to."

Tony could feel the frustration building in the silence that followed. He sighed, his eyes narrowing as he studied Simon’s expressionless face. “Talk to me, man. I’m pulling teeth over here,” Tony pushed, the concern in his voice genuine but edged with a hint of impatience.

Simon grew impatient with Tony. "Dude, I feel like shit, that's all."

Tony let the words sit between them for a moment, before leaning back in his chair. "You should," he said bluntly, not sugarcoating the reality. "You’ve been fucked up for a while."

Simon shifted uncomfortably, the words cutting deeper than he expected. "I got a lot on my mind," he muttered, trying to sound nonchalant, but his voice betrayed him.

Tony shook his head, his voice firm but still gentle. "You should only have two things on your mind: getting better and my sister."

Simon let out a small scoff, rolling his eyes as he leaned back in his chair, trying to shake off the sting of Tony's words. "Whatever," he mumbled, his defenses rising.

But Tony wasn't letting it slide. He leaned forward again, the intensity in his eyes catching Simon off guard. "You know what I told her when you two first started dating?" Tony's voice held a sharp edge of conviction. "I told her that if I could choose anyone for her, I'd choose you."

Simon looked up, his brow furrowed, surprised by Tony's admission.

Tony continued, his voice dropping to a near whisper. "She won't tell me much, 'cause we're bros, but I know, Simon. I know what's been going on. And, man, you're too smart to be this stupid."

The words hit Simon hard. He opened his mouth to respond, but no words came out. Frustration bubbled up inside him, mixing with the guilt and self-loathing that had been gnawing at him for weeks. Did Tony come back just to give him this lecture? To remind him of all the ways he was failing?

"Did you come back just to whip my ass or what?" Simon snapped, his voice sharper than intended.

Tony didn't flinch. He held Simon's gaze, his expression unwavering. "You fuckin' wrecked your bike, man," Tony said, his voice calm but firm. "You didn't have a bomb go off and blow your shit up. I've seen guys with real problems not go off the deep end like you. Stop feeling sorry for yourself and get your shit together."

The truth of Tony's words sank into Simon's chest. He could feel the blood rushing to his face, his hands gripping the edge of the table as if holding on for balance. The words burned because he knew they were right. He had been spiraling, using his pain and injuries as an excuse to keep falling deeper into his addiction, to keep pushing Angie further away.

Tony stood up, tossing the rest of his burrito into the trash. "Get your shit together," he repeated, this time less like an order and more like a plea.

Simon felt the frustration building inside him, the pressure pushing against his ribs. He grabbed his uneaten burrito and followed Tony to the trash can. Without thinking, he tossed it into the trash with more force than necessary, watching as it hit the pile of wrappers and plastic forks.

"Yeah, I got it," Simon muttered, the frustration simmering just beneath his voice.

Tony turned to face him. "I'm not here to make you feel worse, man. I'm here because I still believe in you. And Ang ie... she does too. But you gotta start believing in yourself."

Simon didn't respond. He couldn't. His failures, his addiction, and the wreckage of his life all draped down on him like a cloak. All he could do was nod, hoping that somehow, Tony's words would reach the part of him that still wanted to fight, that still believed in getting better.

But right now, standing in the busy crowd of Coralie's, Simon felt like he was sinking.

Forty-Six

Grown-Up Like

The park was serene, a gentle breeze carrying the scent of freshly cut grass and the distant sounds of kids playing. Simon sat at one of the picnic tables, his fingers tapping lightly against the wood. He looked different, healthier, more put together. The dark circles under his eyes had faded, his skin wasn't as pale, and for the first time in what felt like forever, there was a spark of life behind his eyes. He adjusted the tie around his neck, still getting used to the feel of being dressed in something other than jeans and a hoodie. The crisp slacks and collared shirt made him feel... almost normal again.

Johnny approached the table, his steps casual, a cigarette dangling from his lips. His eyes scanned Simon up and down, a smirk tugging at the corners of his mouth.

"What's with the threads, man?" Johnny asked, taking a seat across from him, blowing out a puff of smoke.

"I just had an interview," Simon replied, his voice steady, a small sense of pride creeping into his tone.

Johnny raised an eyebrow. "For where, man?"

"Big Five," Simon said, shrugging like it wasn't a big deal but it had been a long time since Simon had felt like he had something to strive for. A real chance.

Johnny leaned back in his chair, flicking ash from his cigarette. "Big Five, huh? Selling sports shit? You really think that's your vibe, bro?"

Simon chuckled, but his smile was tight. "I think it's better than what I've been doing, Johnny."

Johnny shrugged, the moment already forgotten as he leaned in, eyes gleaming with the real question on his mind. "So did you score some magic beans or what?"

Simon's expression hardened, the lightness fading from his face. He reached into his pocket and pulled out a small Altoids tin, placing it on the table in front of Johnny.

Johnny raised an eyebrow, snatching the tin up quickly. He popped it open, expecting a treasure trove, but his face fell when he saw the meager contents inside. "That's it?"

Simon nodded, his voice firm. "It's the last of my stash. I'm out."

Johnny closed the tin, shaking his head in disbelief. "What the hell am I gonna do, man?"

Simon leaned forward, his eyes locking with Johnny's. "You're a grown-ass man, Johnny. Walk into Urgent Care, hit up Fish or Freddy. You know the drill. I'm done."

Johnny's expression shifted from disbelief to irritation, but deep down, there was a flicker of something else, worry. He hadn't expected this from Simon. They'd always been in it together, running the same cycle of highs and lows, but now... Simon was out. "Fish is out, man. Freddy's girl just had a baby. He's all tied up."

Simon smirked slightly. “Good for them. Maybe it’s time you get tied up in some real life, too.”

Johnny stood up, frustration etched across his face as he pocketed the tin. “Balls, man. Fuckin' balls.”

Simon watched him go. He knew it wasn’t going to be easy to let go of the life he had been living, the people who had been part of it for so long. But that wasn’t who he wanted to be anymore. This was a fresh start, he could feel it.

“Hey!” Simon called after Johnny as he started walking away. Johnny turned back, an annoyed look on his face. “Can you drop me off at my pad?”

Johnny sighed, flicking his cigarette butt to the ground as he motioned toward his car. "Where's your truck?"

Simon’s jaw clenched, the memory of the crash still vivid in his mind. "Wrecked it, dumbass."

Johnny chuckled as the two of them walked toward the car. “Oh right. That's why you're walking.”

"Yeah," Simon replied, his tone dry. "That and my license is suspended."

They both got into Johnny’s beat-up car, the smell of old fast food and cigarettes filling the space. As they drove, Simon stared out the window, watching the streets blur by, thinking about how far he'd come. He didn’t have all the answers. Hell, he didn’t even know how the job interview had gone. But there was something inside him that had shifted, a determination he hadn’t felt in a long time.

He was done with the magic beans. Done with the pills. Done with the lies. This was his shot to rebuild, to take control of his life again, and for once, Simon felt like he wasn’t going to let it slip away.

As Johnny drove in silence, Simon leaned his head against the window and closed his eyes. He knew the road ahead wasn't going to be easy, but for the first time in a long time, he wasn't afraid of the fight.

FORTY-SEVEN

BREAKING DOWN, BREAKING THROUGH

Simon sat on the crinkling paper of the exam table, his hands resting on his lap, fingers twitching anxiously. The sterile smell of the doctor's office clung to the air, amplifying the tension between him and Angie. He kept his eyes forward, fixated on the blank wall across from him, though the faint reflection of the X-rays and MRI scans on the wall-mounted light box caught his peripheral vision. His mind buzzed with fragmented thoughts, and though he tried to focus on the present, everything felt dull beneath the surface.

Dr. Gifford, a middle-aged man with salt-and-pepper hair and kind eyes, was leaning over the images, frowning slightly as he traced his finger along a specific point on the MRI. Angie sat nearby, her body taut with nervous energy, her eyes darting between Simon and the doctor, waiting for some kind of answer, some glimmer of hope.

Dr. Gifford straightened up. "Well, the X-ray is inconclusive," he began, his voice measured, calm. "Which is why I ordered the MRI. Now that we've got it done, we can see right here," he pointed at a faint line on the scan, "on your tailbone. There's a fracture. See this? That's likely been causing you all that pain and discomfort."

Simon blinked, his eyes tracking the doctor's finger as it moved over the small, barely visible line on the image. A fracture. He should've felt relieved, validated even. There was a reason for the pain after all. He wasn't imagining it. But instead of relief, a numbness settled over him like a thick fog, suffocating any real emotion.

"Can it be fixed?" Simon's voice was flat, almost devoid of curiosity. He knew what was coming next.

Dr. Gifford offered a small, sympathetic smile. "Fixed? No. But it can be removed. That's what I'd recommend."

Angie shifted in her seat, leaning forward, her hands clasped tightly in her lap as if she was holding onto something fragile. "Removed?" she asked, her tone both cautious and hopeful. "And that would help the pain?"

Dr. Gifford nodded. "I believe so. Removing it should significantly reduce the pain, if not eliminate it altogether."

The words hung in the air for a moment, settling between Simon and Angie like an unspoken question. Could it really be that simple? Could all of this, years of pain, years of numbing himself with pills and chasing temporary relief, finally have a solution?

Simon rubbed his hands over his jeans, feeling the rough fabric against his palms. "How soon could it be done?" he asked, though his voice was distant, unsure how to take in the hope of a solution.

Dr. Gifford glanced at his tablet. "Probably in a couple of weeks. We'll get you on the books as soon as we can. Recovery should take about one to two weeks, depending on how quickly you heal."

Angie's heart lifted slightly. This was it. The answer they'd been waiting for, praying for. The chance for Simon to finally get better, to leave the pain and the pills behind. Her mind raced ahead, imagining the possibilities, the life they could have once Simon was free from the constant ache. She could almost see it, that version of him who existed before the accident, before everything spiraled out of control.

The doctor's voice cut through her thoughts. "Please, take some time to think it over. You have my email if any questions come up."

Simon nodded, but the motion felt mechanical, as if he was going through the motions of being present but was really somewhere far away. "Thanks, doc," he muttered, sliding off the exam table with a stiffness that had nothing to do with his back.

Dr. Gifford smiled kindly at Angie as he left the room. "We'll see you soon," he said before closing the door behind him.

As soon as the door clicked shut, Angie turned toward Simon, her excitement barely contained. "What do you think? That's good, right?" Her eyes searched his face, looking for any sign that he shared her relief, that he felt the same spark of hope that was burning inside her.

But Simon didn't respond. He just stared at her for a long moment, his face unreadable, before turning on his heel and walking out of the exam room without a word.

"Simon?" Angie called after him, confusion knotting in her stomach. She scrambled out of her chair, hurrying after him, her heart pounding with an unfamiliar mixture of dread and desperation. She caught up with him just outside the clinic, grabbing his arm lightly, trying to keep her voice steady. "Simon, what's wrong? Talk to me."

He pulled his arm away, his jaw clenched. "I need air, Ang. Just... let me breathe for a second."

She stopped in her tracks, watching as he moved away from her, the distance between them growing not just physically, but in ways she couldn't quite grasp. How could he not see what this meant? Why wasn't he as relieved as she was?

This was supposed to be the turning point, wasn't it? The beginning of something better. But as she stood there, watching Simon walk ahead of her, his shoulders hunched and his head down, she couldn't help but feel like they were still stuck, no matter how many answers they found.

The hallway stretched out before them, sterile and silent, the fluorescent lights above glared down on them. Simon didn't slow down, his steps growing more hurried as they approached the elevator. He jabbed the down arrow, the glowing button lighting up under his finger, but the screen above the doors showed that the elevator was on the second floor. It might as well have been a mile away.

Simon shifted restlessly, everything they'd just heard in the doctor's office was like an invisible hand tightening around his throat. He didn't wait for the elevator. His feet moved on instinct, finding the door to the stairwell instead, the sound of it slamming shut behind him echoed through the empty corridor. Angie barely had time to react, her heart lurching as she hurried after him.

The echo of their footsteps filled the stairwell, Simon's quick and erratic, Angie's more hesitant as she tried to keep up, unsure of what was driving him to move so quickly away from her, from them, from everything. Her breath came faster, not just from the stairs but from the rising panic that threatened to overtake her. She wasn't sure what was happening, was this another outburst, another way to deflect, or was something deeper unraveling inside him?

As they rounded another flight, a woman in a white coat crossed their path, likely another doctor on her way to some other appointment. Simon stopped abruptly, his hand shooting out to get her attention.

"Excuse me, ma'am," Simon's voice came out sharper than he intended, frustration and exhaustion behind it. "What would you do if I told you I think I'm having a heart attack?"

The woman froze mid-step, her eyes wide with concern as she took him in. "Sir, are you having a heart attack?"

"No," Simon said, the word hanging in the air between them like a bitter joke. "But if I said that, you wouldn't, I don't know, examine my feet, would you?"

The doctor blinked, visibly puzzled, unsure of how to respond to such an odd question. "I... I'm sorry?"

"Yeah," Simon muttered, already turning away, shaking his head as though he'd confirmed something only he understood. "Thought so."

He continued down the stairs without another word, leaving the woman standing there, bewildered. Angie rushed past, offering a helpless shrug as an apology to the doctor, unsure how to explain Simon's behavior.

"I don't know," Angie said, almost to herself, totally confused. "I'm sorry."

By the time they reached the lobby, Simon was already pushing through the glass doors, heading toward the building's exit like he was trying to outrun something. It wasn't just the news they'd received but something deeper, something rawer. Angie had seen it in him before, that look, that need to escape from what he couldn't control, but this felt different.

She couldn't keep up with it, couldn't catch the pieces fast enough before they slipped through her fingers.

Simon was talking, but not to her. His words were loud enough for her to hear, but it was like he was speaking into the void, airing out grievances that had long been buried under years of pain and dismissal.

"Shit," he muttered, his voice a mix of bitterness and frustration. "Do you know how many doctors haven't believed me? How many told me to my face that I was making it all up?"

The venom in his voice sent a shiver down Angie's spine. She had seen him defeated before, but never quite like this. His anger wasn't explosive. It was quiet, simmering under the surface, and it scared her more than any outburst ever could.

As Simon held the door open for a man in a white coat carrying vials of blood, he didn't miss a beat. "Let me ask you something, man. Do you get bonuses for writing scripts?"

The lab tech blinked, confused, clearly caught off guard. "I'm a lab tech, so... no."

"Good for you," Simon muttered, walking away before the man could say anything else, leaving him as puzzled as the woman in the stairwell.

Angie followed closely behind, her mind tumbling. She wanted to ask him what the hell was happening, to ask why he wasn't relieved after they had finally gotten an answer. A real answer to his pain. Wasn't this what they had been waiting for? Wasn't this the turning point?

She stayed silent, following him out into the afternoon light towards their car, her heart aching for him.

The parking lot sprawled out before them, cars lined up in neat rows, but Simon's mind was far from orderly. He marched ahead with Angie close behind, her footsteps tapping in rhythm with the pounding of his emotions. He didn't know where they were headed exactly, just that they needed to keep moving. Somewhere. Anywhere. The familiar feeling of being caged clawed at his chest.

"Three C," Angie called out, her voice breaking through the fog of his thoughts. She gestured toward the distant corner of the lot where their car sat waiting like a silent witness.

They weaved through parked cars, climbing the narrow concrete stairs, the silence between them growing heavier. Simon's muscles tensed with every step. He could feel the frustration, the anger, and the guilt all bubbling up inside him like a dam ready to burst. His mind replayed every word from the doctor's office on an endless loop, and it felt like his heart was on fire.

"They told me I was changing my story," Simon growled suddenly, his voice shaking. "Didn't even take the time to *listen* or *look* at my medical record. They gave me pills, so I took 'em." He jumped up, slapping the concrete beam above him. Then, without thinking, he started shadow boxing the air. Punching at the invisible enemy that had been haunting him for years. Every hit was filled with rage, with helplessness.

Angie stopped in her tracks, watching him. This wasn't the Simon she was used to, the bottled-up, sarcastic Simon who hid his pain behind his jokes. This was unleashed.

"Simon, hold up," Angie called out, her voice pleading with him to slow down, to breathe. But he was past that.

"What, Ang? What?" He turned to face her, his eyes wild. "I've heard it a thousand times. 'Simon, you're a pill-poppin' junkie.' 'Get your shit together.' It's not *all* my fault!" His voice cracked with his confession. "It doesn't take much to get hooked on that shit, you know? But no doctor told me that. Not one. No one warned me. I was hooked before the first damn bottle was dry. I didn't even *know it*."

He let out a hollow laugh, bitter and broken. "My *drug-dealing buddy* was the one who told me. He could relate."

They were near the car now, the tension between them crackling like static in the air. Angie stood by quietly, her heart aching as she took in the sight of Simon, fists still clenched at his sides. His outburst caught her off guard. She didn't know how to reach him in a moment like this, but she had to try.

Simon wasn't done. He was on the verge of breaking. His pain behind it was razor-sharp. "This doctor today was the first one to *look at me*. He actually wants to help. He *proved* I'm not a total fuck-up. I've had a legit injury for years now, Ang. I'm not a fake. I'm not a totally fucked up."

"I know you're not," Angie whispered, stepping closer. She wanted to comfort him, to wrap him in her arms.

Simon shook his head, his voice hoarse. "And you know what the kicker is? That's only *half* the problem."

Angie moved toward him, reaching out, but just as her fingers brushed his arm, Simon's phone rang. The sound was sharp, jarring, like a needle scratching across vinyl. Simon glanced at the screen, and without a word, he turned and walked a few steps away to answer it. Angie stood by the car, her hand falling to her side.

As Simon talked on the phone, his face darkened, and Angie could sense the shift in him. Whatever was happening on the other end of that call wasn't good. She got into the driver's seat and watched him.

Moments later, Simon ended the call and walked back to the car. He got into the passenger seat without a word.

She put the key in the ignition. Before she could say anything, Simon slammed his phone against the dashboard with a force that made her jump. The crack echoed through the car, and Angie froze, her breath catching in her throat.

Simon put his head in his hands, his body trembling as a muffled yell broke free. His sobs were raw and unfiltered, the sound of a man who had been pushed to his limit. Angie's heart clenched at the sight of him unraveling, and for a moment, she didn't know what to do. She had never seen him like this.

"Si..." she whispered, her voice tentative. "What's going on?"

He didn't look up, but his voice came through, broken and strained. "The insurance guy called," he choked out. "The other driver was injured... he can't really say how bad."

Angie hadn't thought much about the other person in the crash and hadn't wanted to.

Simon wiped at his face with the back of his hand, but it didn't stop the tears. "I could've killed us, Angie. And I don't even remember the crash. I... I messed this guy up. He could have a family, a life. What if... what if he ends up like me? What if I made him like me?"

His words hung in the air, filled with guilt, fear, and exhaustion. Angie felt tears well up in her own eyes as she watched him. For so long, Simon had been fighting this battle with his addiction, with his pain, and now, he was drowning in the consequences.

"I'm so tired of this, babe," Simon whispered, his voice barely audible. "I'm so tired of everything."

Angie's heart ached for him. She reached out, her hand finding his. Her fingers wrapped around his tightly, holding on, offering him the only thing she could in that moment: her presence.

Simon turned his head, his tear-streaked face looking at her with a mixture of guilt and relief. He squeezed her hand, and in that silent moment, something shifted between them. It wasn't forgiveness or a solution, but it was them, a thread of connection in the mess of everything that had come between them.

They sat there for a long time, hand in hand, the world outside the car continuing on while they stayed locked in their shared pain. Angie knew there was no easy fix, no sudden resolution. But Simon was finally allowing himself to feel, to be vulnerable. And that was a step she wasn't going to let him take alone.

Forty-Eight

Who Needs a Plan Anyway?

Evening shadows stretched long as Angie pulled the car into a familiar driveway. The air between her and Simon felt lighter than it had in weeks, as if the unspoken worries had lifted, just for a moment. Simon sat next to her, dressed neatly in slacks and a button-up shirt, just done with a full shift at Big 5, looking healthier than he had in a long time. His hair, combed back with some effort, made him look like the man she fell in love with before everything got tangled in pills and pain.

She kept her eyes on the house, Simon's childhood home, as her fingers tapped nervously on the steering wheel. The last time they'd been here, everything had felt different, more strained. Now, there was still an unease beneath her skin, but it was laced with something else. Hope, maybe.

"You sure you want to just stop by?" Angie asked, her voice filled with hesitation.

Simon, still gripping her hand like an anchor, nodded. "It'll be fine."

The confidence in his voice was shaky, but he held on to it. He gave her hand a reassuring squeeze before letting go and stepping out of the car. Angie followed suit, watching as he adjusted his collar before walking up the front steps. He hesitated for the briefest second before pressing the doorbell.

A moment later, the door swung open, revealing Jared, his brother, still as brash and unfiltered as ever.

"Hey, Simon. Angie," Jared greeted, his voice casual, almost indifferent.

"What up, Jared," Simon replied, forcing a grin that didn't quite meet his eyes.

Angie offered a polite, "Hi," as they stepped inside, feeling the familiar pull of awkwardness as they crossed the threshold. The smell of crunchy tacos and seasoned meat wafted through the air, and the sound of conversation between Susan and Hank floated toward them from the dining area.

Susan and Hank were just setting down plates of food on the table, preparing for dinner. The sight of Simon caught them off guard, and for a moment, the air was thick with an unspoken tension. It was the first time Simon had come to see them since everything had spiraled out of control. Their smiles were slow to form, unsure, almost as if they didn't quite know how to react to the sight of their son standing there. Healthier but still marked by all that had happened.

"Hi, son," Hank greeted, stepping forward cautiously. "Come in."

Susan's voice was warmer, though still tinged with hesitation. "Oh, hey you two. You want to join us for dinner?"

Simon shook his head gently. "Uh, no thanks, Mom. We can't stay long."

They all stood there for a moment, the four of them around the dining table, like statues waiting for someone to break the stillness. Jared, however, had no qualms about shattering the silence, already seated at the table, serving himself a taco.

"I just wanted to tell you," Simon started, his voice low, "I'll be having surgery soon. I had an MRI done, and the doctor said my tailbone is fractured. That's what's been causing all the pain. So... they're going to remove it."

Susan's hands fluttered to her chest, her motherly instinct kicking in. "When does that happen?"

Angie chimed in, trying to help ease the conversation. "We haven't confirmed the date yet, but they said soon."

"That's good news," Hank said, the relief evident in his voice. "That's great. You look good."

"Yeah, I've been working on it," Simon replied, shifting awkwardly on his feet.

Jared, never one to miss an opportunity for a jab, piped up. "Why you dressed up? Did you have a court date?"

"Jared," Susan scolded, though her voice lacked any real firmness.

"What?" Jared shrugged, grinning. "We're all thinking it."

Simon sighed but managed to keep his composure. "No, I work at Big Five now."

Jared looked unimpressed as he reached for the shredded cheese. "Why dress up? I don't get it, you're sporting goods."

Simon passed the cheese to Jared without comment, shaking his head at the absurdity of the question.

"That's good," Susan said, trying to fill the awkward space. "That's really good, Simon."

Simon nodded, his eyes downcast. "That's all, really. I just wanted to tell you guys. Now we know I wasn't faking the injury and I'm not a total loser."

"Simon," Hank interjected, a hint of sadness in his voice.

But Simon kept going, his words tumbling out like they had been waiting to escape for too long. "It's okay, Dad. I know where my fault lies. You guys have helped us a lot. You've always been there. And... thank you for that."

Jared crunched into his taco loudly, oblivious to the atmosphere around him.

"We never thought you were faking it, Simon," Hank said, his voice gruff with emotion. "We saw the bruising on your body. You think I'll ever forget that? You were here. We were here for you."

"It was so gross, man," Jared added, completely missing the gravity of the moment.

Susan's eyes were on the verge of tears. "We were here to care for you. We did everything we could. Why do you..."

But Simon cut her off, his voice thick with guilt. "I'm the one who's let you down. I'm the one who wrecked my bike and turned all our lives to shit. I'm sorry."

There was a long pause, Simon's apology hanging heavily in the room. Susan's eyes filled with tears, and she stepped forward, her voice trembling. "Simon, honey... We're sorry too. We're sorry we couldn't see how bad things were getting."

Jared's loud crunching cut through the tension once again, and Hank shot him a look. "Simon, you're not a disappointment. We didn't know how to manage it all. You sure as hell couldn't. We didn't know how to help. We had to let go for you. Jared, shut up."

"Sorry," Jared mumbled, slowing down his chewing.

Simon let out a deep breath, the heaviness of everything he had held inside finally starting to lift. "Well, we gotta go," he said quietly. "I'll let you know the date."

Susan wiped at her eyes. "We can help you if you need it. I'd like to help."

Simon gave her a small, sad smile. "Yeah, we'll see, Mom. It's fine. It's not a major surgery. Anyways, have a good night."

As Simon turned toward the door, Angie followed, her heart aching for the fragility of this moment between Simon and his family. Just as they reached the door, Jared spoke up again, his voice casual as if the last few minutes hadn't happened.

"Won't they load you up with pills again after surgery?" he asked. "Like, isn't that how it works?"

Simon stiffened but didn't turn around. "Yeah, maybe."

"So... what's the point?" Jared pressed, his voice dripping with doubt.

Angie stepped in, her voice firm. "Why not give him the benefit of the doubt, huh?"

Simon shrugged, his voice quiet but resolved. "Relapse is part of getting better. I'm trying to be better. I'm just telling you in case... you know, in case something happens."

Hank's voice broke through the unease. "You'll be fine, Simon. You'll be just fine."

Simon nodded, though the doubt lingered in his eyes. "Sure," he muttered, then turned toward the door. "But just in case... I love you all."

The words hung in the air. As he opened the door and stepped out, Angie lingered, looking back to see the conflicting emotions etched on Hank's and Susan's faces. Jared, oblivious, was already halfway through another taco, barely glancing up.

Angie took a breath, her voice soft but steady. "I know this hasn't been easy on any of us, and I'm sorry for not seeing how I've enabled him. But he *is* trying, and I know he really misses you." She looked directly at Jared. "Even you, Jared."

Jared paused mid-bite, a flicker of something. Maybe recognition or surprise crossed his face. But he said nothing, simply nodding.

The night air outside the Wagner home was cool. The awkward tension from inside still clung to them, unresolved and lingering in the silence between them. Angie glanced at Simon, sensing the tightness in his shoulders.

"That was a bit of a doozy," Angie said.

Simon exhaled deeply, rubbing the back of his neck. "That's not what I was really hoping for," he muttered, a touch of disappointment in his voice.

Angie stopped, reaching out to take his hand, forcing him to pause and face her. She stepped closer, her eyes searching his.

"Simon," she began, "you need your family. We need your family. There's always going to be stuff to work out, but you need them."

He stared down at her, the words sinking in even as he tried to fight them. He knew she was right. He knew he needed them, despite the awkwardness, the distance, and the unresolved pain. But the admission wasn't easy. It never had been.

"I know," he finally said, his voice low, barely above a whisper.

Without another word, he wrapped his arm around her shoulders and kissed the top of her head. Angie closed her eyes, leaning into him, feeling his warmth, his familiar scent, and the way his presence always grounded her, despite everything.

Forty-Nine

Overthinking Everything

The sun was already high in the sky, casting a golden light across the loading dock as Angie stood, cradling her cup of coffee. The warmth of the morning didn't reach the anxiety twisting inside her. She stared out at the street, lost in her thoughts, her mind racing over the same worry again and again.

The creak of the dock door caught her attention, and she turned to see Benjamin, his familiar, easy smile greeting her as he walked up.

"It's a beautiful morning," Benjamin said, his voice cheerful.

Angie managed a small smile. "Yes, indeed."

He studied her for a moment, sensing the tension in her posture. "Why are you so nervous?"

Angie hesitated, her grip tightening on the coffee cup. She hadn't planned on unloading everything, but Benjamin had a way of reading her, cutting through her defenses with that quiet, steady presence. She sighed, taking a deep breath before answering.

"Simon's surgery is tomorrow," she said, her voice more vulnerable than she intended. "I'm feeling all kinds of things. It shouldn't be that big of a deal, but..."

"But it is," Benjamin finished for her, his brow furrowing in concern.

Angie nodded. She hadn't said it aloud yet, but the fear had been gnawing at her for days, creeping in every time she thought about the surgery.

"It's... 'that moment,' you know?" she began slowly, "It feels like the final crossroad. We're curing one piece, but that pull, that pull is always there. Is he stronger than it? And then relapse..." Her voice wavered, the uncertainty, the fear all rushing up at once. "I get it. I know it's going to happen. They all say it. But if he drowns again, Benny..."

Her voice trailed off. She felt exposed, raw, like she had just peeled back a layer of herself she hadn't meant to share.

Benjamin, ever the steady anchor, placed a gentle hand on her shoulder, pulling her into a comforting side hug. His presence, reminding her that she didn't have to face this fear alone.

"I know," he said quietly, his voice steady and reassuring. "Time can feel more like an enemy than a friend sometimes."

Angie leaned into him, letting her head rest on his shoulder, the moment of vulnerability washing over her like a wave. "Yeah," she whispered. The uncertainty, the nagging question of whether Simon was truly ready to fight the addiction once and for all.

Benjamin squeezed her shoulder gently, "Day by day, kid," he said. "You're not alone in this either."

"Thank you," Angie closed her eyes, letting a fragile sense of peace wrap around her. It wasn't much, but it was enough to keep going.

FIFTY

LIVING ON A PRAYER

The wooden doors of Sacred Heart creaked as they opened, letting in a sliver of light. Angie stepped inside, her footsteps quiet against the cool stone floor. This church, where she and Simon were married, was a place that had always offered her solace, a sacred space where the chaos of the outside world seemed to melt away.

Angie dipped her fingers into the holy water font near the entrance, tracing the sign of the cross over herself with a quiet reverence. She needed the quiet, the grounding, the connection to something bigger than herself. Something that made her feel less alone.

The church wasn't empty, but it was quiet. A few other souls dotted the pews, heads bowed, hands clasped in prayer. Some murmured under their breath, others were lost in their own silent conversations with God. Angie made her way to one of the pews and knelt down.

The silence of the church wrapped around her like a protective cocoon, offering her a moment of stillness, the ability to surrender her struggles, her fears, to God. And today, she needed that connection more than ever.

Her mind wandered as she knelt there, flickering between memories of Simon. She wanted him back. Not just sober, but whole. She wanted to believe that it was possible, that they could both make it through this. But doubt was a relentless force, creeping into her heart even as she prayed.

"Help me help him. Help me find the strength." She seemed to have this simple prayer on repeat these days.

As she knelt in the stillness, lost in her thoughts, she didn't notice Fr. Charles approach until she felt his presence beside her. His footsteps had been soft, and as she glanced up, she was greeted by his warm, gentle smile.

"Hi Angie," he said, as if not to disturb the quiet reverence of the space.

She blinked, caught off guard by his presence but somehow comforted. "Hello Father, I wouldn't expect to find you here...I mean at Sacred Heart", she laughed.

"I just happen to be helping out Fr. Peter today. How are you holding up?" he asked.

Angie had always appreciated Fr. Charles. He had a way of grounding people, of meeting them where they were with kindness and understanding. She gave him a small smile, though it wavered. "I'm trying, Father. I'm really trying."

Fr. Charles nodded, his expression thoughtful, as he sat down on the pew next to her. His demeanor was casual, yet there was always a wisdom behind his relaxed approach. He leaned back slightly, letting the silence fill the gap between them for a moment. "God knows how hard you've been trying,

Angie. And He hears every prayer, even the ones you don't have the words for."

The tears that welled up were out of gratitude for the people she had around her, "Thank you, Father," she whispered.

"Keep praying. Keep trusting. And know that no matter what happens, He is with you, always. You're stronger than you think, Angie."

She nodded, her shoulders feeling just a little lighter, Fr. Charles stood, giving her one last encouraging smile before heading back toward the altar.

A few minutes later, as she made her way toward the exit. She said one final prayer for Simon and for them. Then, she left the church, the echo of her whispered prayers following her into the afternoon light.

She didn't have all the answers, she didn't need to. The comfort of her faith was guidance enough.

Fifty-One

Putting On a Brave Face

The waiting room was cold, sterile, and filled with the energy that came with waiting for news. Angie sat beside her father, flipping through a worn magazine, though her eyes barely registered the glossy pages. Articles about recipes, celebrity gossip, and home improvement tips blurred into one another, their words meaningless. Every so often, she'd glance at the clock on the wall, watching the minutes crawl by.

Next to her, Edgar sat hunched over in his chair, engrossed in a paperback crime novel. His weathered hands held the book firmly, though his eyes would flick up from the pages now and again, darting toward the door. Angie knew her father wasn't really as calm as he seemed. He was waiting, just like her. They all were.

The smell of antiseptic lingered in the air, a reminder of where they were. Surgery that was supposed to be simple and routine, but with Simon the worry was always close to the surface.

Edgar shifted in his seat, marking his place in the book with his thumb before closing it with a *thud*. He exhaled. Angie glanced up at him, noticing the way his brows furrowed slightly, a sure sign he was deep in thought.

"Mija," he began, his voice quiet but steady, "I don't say it often, but I'm proud of you."

Angie blinked, taken aback. It wasn't that her father was withholding his emotions. His compliments, when they came, always felt earned. "Really?" she asked, a smile forming as she looked into his tired eyes. "Um, thank you, Dad."

Edgar nodded, as he continued, "I know things have been tough, and I can see how hard it's been on you, but you've held on. You've done everything you could, even when it feels like it's all falling apart. I'm proud of you for that. For not giving up."

It was hard to feel proud of herself, to feel like she was doing anything right in the midst of the chaos that had become her life. But hearing it from her father, someone who had lived through his own struggles and heartbreaks, it felt different. It felt real.

"Thanks, Dad," she said, her voice quieter now, almost shy. "I think I'm a bit stubborn, like you."

Edgar chuckled, a sound that warmed her heart. "Maybe," he said, tilting his head slightly, as if considering her words. "But you got *ganas*, mija. You're a fighter. I see that."

Angie nodded, feeling a sense of peace settle over her, he was right. She had fought and was still fighting, for Simon, for their life together.

Before she could respond, the sound of footsteps approaching drew their attention. Susan and Hank entered the waiting room. Susan carried a tray of coffees, her hands steady despite the worry that had etched itself into the lines of her face.

"Hi, Angie," Susan greeted warmly, offering one of the coffees with a warm smile. "We thought it was about time for some coffee."

Angie smiled, taking the cup gratefully. "Oh, yes, thank you," she replied, feeling the warmth of the cup seep into her hands. "I'm glad you're here."

Hank gave a small nod to Edgar, extending his hand. "Edgar, nice to see you again."

Edgar stood to shake Hank's hand, his demeanor calm but respectful. "Same to you, Hank."

They all settled into their seats, the air around them thick with anticipation. Susan sat beside Angie, offering a reassuring smile, but the anxiety was clear in the lines of her forehead, the way her eyes darted toward the door every few minutes.

Finally, after what seemed like an eternity, the door opened, and Dr. Gifford entered the waiting room. His presence was calm, his expression neutral but kind. He approached them with the ease of someone who had done this a hundred times before.

"Everything went well," Dr. Gifford said, his voice steady and reassuring. "The surgery was successful, and Simon is in recovery now. He'll be groggy for a bit, but everything looks good."

There was a collective sigh of relief. "Thank you," she whispered, although it felt like it wasn't enough. Gratitude swelled in her heart.

Dr. Gifford gave them a small smile before excusing himself, leaving the family to absorb the news.

Later that evening, they gathered in Simon's hospital room. The television illuminated the room, casting a warm, comforting light over the scene. Simon lay in bed, propped up on his side, his face pale but relaxed. He was surrounded by his parents, Angie, and Edgar, all of them laughing quietly at the *Seinfeld* episode playing on the screen.

As the night wore on, Simon drifted into a deep sleep, the rhythm of his breathing filling the quiet room. Angie curled up on the semi-futon nearby. She watched him sleep for a while, her heart full of hope and of a new beginning.

Fifty-Two

Time Will Tell

The apartment was bathed in a muted light, the kind that filtered through the curtains on a hazy afternoon. Dust particles floated lazily in the air, suspended in a kind of quiet stillness. Susan moved about the small space with practiced ease, carrying a lunch tray in her hands as she made her way toward Simon's bed. Her footsteps were soft, deliberate, almost cautious, as if she was tiptoeing around an unspoken tension.

On the other side of the room, Hank stood with a hammer in hand, carefully hanging the wedding frames that had been resting against the wall for months. The clink of the hammer against nails echoed in the otherwise quiet apartment.

The conversation had disappeared as the door clicked shut behind Susan and Hank, leaving Simon alone in the quiet apartment. The warmth they tried to bring with the lunch tray and Hank's efforts to finally hang up the wedding frames on the wall evaporated the moment they left. Now, the room felt still, almost hollow, the kind of silence that made every tick of the clock sound too loud.

Simon's fragile mask of composure cracked. He moved with sudden urgency, the bed protesting with a loud creak as he swung his legs over the edge. Standing too quickly, dizziness rushed over him, leaving him momentarily unsteady. The pain in his body was different now. No longer the chronic ache he had learned to endure. These were fresh, sharp pains from the surgery, a new kind of discomfort that gnawed at him. Dr. Gifford had been careful with the post-op meds, giving Simon just enough to manage the pain without spiraling back. But the small dose only teased him, leaving his hunger for more wide open.

First, the bathroom cabinet. Nothing. The sock drawer came next. Simon dug through the mismatched socks and old receipts, hoping to find something that would take the edge off. But it was empty. His secret stash, the place he had always counted on, was bone dry.

He moved toward the closet. His last hope. A shoebox, hidden away at the very back, had once been a treasure trove, a place where he had hidden pills for a rainy day.

Empty.

This was a moment of truth for Simon, one of many he knew were still ahead. The temptation pulled at him like an old lover, his "med mistress" beckoning him to fall back into her arms. But now, he faced the choice. Would he surrender, or was he finally strong enough to resist?

Fifty-Three

Now You Get It

Meanwhile, across town, Angie wandered the bright aisles of a bridal shop, immersed in the lightness of the moment. Dresses of every style and fabric draped along racks, creating an atmosphere of celebration and hope. She ran her fingers across the fabrics, feeling the textures beneath her fingertips as her mind drifted to the present, Rosie's wedding.

Rosie came bounding down the aisle, dress in hand, her excitement contagious.

"Look, something like this?" Rosie held up a simple gown, the beaded detail catching a sparkle in the lighting.

Angie smiled, taking in her sister's happiness. "Oh, that's pretty. I could see you in that," she said, warmth filling her voice.

Sofia, who had been wandering nearby, nodded. "Yes, *mija*, that's perfect."

Rosie, with an excited bounce in her step, headed toward the fitting rooms. "This makes seven," she beamed. "I think that's a good start."

Angie chuckled, watching her sister disappear behind the dressing room door. "Let the show begin."

She and Sofia took a seat just outside, waiting patiently, the excitement of the store enveloping them.

From behind the curtain, Rosie's voice emerged, tinged with disbelief, "I can't believe I'm trying on wedding dresses."

"I can't either," Sofia responded, reflecting on the bittersweet moment. "Both of my *mijitas* will be married. I'm happy and feel old at the same time."

Angie smiled, catching the nostalgia in their mother's tone. "You're not old, Ma."

Sofia laughed, but there was a tenderness to her words. "I'm getting up there."

Angie looked toward the fitting room, her mind momentarily pulled back to Simon. She pushed the thought away, focusing on Rosie's moment. "Try the fitted one, the off-shoulder with the lace."

"Your favorite?" Rosie teased.

"I just think it suits you."

The door clicked open, and Rosie stepped out onto the raised platform, the simple white gown flowing effortlessly with each step. Her smile was wide, her eyes bright with joy.

"Oh *mija*," Sofia whispered, her voice catching in her throat.

Angie's eyes took in her sister's beauty. "You're glowing. It's beautiful on you."

Rosie beamed, stepping in front of the mirror, the reflection capturing more than just a dress. It was also the happiness she radiated, the love that filled her heart.

"I can't stop smiling," Rosie admitted, wiping at the tears threatening to spill over.

"*Porque estás en la nube*," Sofia said with a playful smile..

"Yep, cloud nine," Angie added, watching as Rosie turned from side to side, admiring the fit of the dress.

Rosie's tears welled, not from the dress itself, but from the love it represented. "I think it's more him than the dress," she confessed, turning toward Angie and Sofia. "The connection with Julio... I can't explain it. My head doesn't have the right words. But I just know, with everything that..."

Angie's gaze locked with Rosie's, and a knowing smile crept onto her face. "That you'd walk to the edge of the earth in like tattered Converse with oozing blisters on your feet and probably gnarly sores on your lips from the sun beating down just to be with him."

Rosie let out a laugh. "Um, that sounds like fun. But yes, I would."

Angie nodded, "Yeah," she whispered, "I get it."

For a moment, they held each other's gaze, a quiet understanding passing between them.

Sofia, watching her daughters, wiped at her eyes again. "See, your inside is always right," she murmured, her voice breaking with emotion. "*Aiy yai yai*. I'm all teary. Beautiful *mija*, just beautiful."

Rosie smiled through her teary eyes, basking in the love and joy that surrounded her.

Fifty-Four

Bridging the Gap

Simon stood in line, a small piece of paper clutched in his hand—a prescription for Oxycodone, crinkled at the edges from his nervous grip. The fluorescent lights overhead buzzed faintly, casting a sterile glow over the scene. The usual drugstore chatter echoed around him; the beeps of cash registers, the idle conversation, the distant rustling of shopping bags. It was a familiar setting, but Simon's mind was far from familiar ground.

He stared down at the script, his eyes tracing the familiar letters, the temptation of it coiling tightly around him like a snake. He knew what that script represented. His escape, a return to the numbing fog that had consumed him for so long. He felt the tug, that insidious pull toward the thing he'd vowed to leave behind. His heart raced, his fingers trembling slightly as he debated what to do next.

As the line inched forward, his eyes drifted toward the nearby display rack. Rows of pamphlets stood silently, their brightly colored covers offering help, guidance, and solutions to all kinds of problems. *AIDS awareness, Diabetes management, Quitting smoking*, but it was another title that caught his eye, one that made his chest tighten. *"Getting Over Opiates: Could Methadone Help You?"*

Simon stepped out of line as if in a trance. He reached for the pamphlet. His eyes skimmed over the title again, the words blurring slightly. *Could methadone help? Was that the next step?* He didn't know. But as he held the pamphlet in his hands, a glimmer of something flickered within him. He folded the pamphlet carefully and slid it into his back pocket, turning his back on the prescription counter and walking out the door.

Fifty-Five

That's Enough for Today

The late afternoon sun bathed Ventura Pier in a golden glow, casting long shadows across the weathered wooden planks beneath Simon's feet. He leaned against the rail, his arms resting on the rough wood as he gazed out at the ocean. The rhythmic crashing of the waves against the pier's supports offered a strange kind of solace, a backdrop to the storm raging inside his mind. The sea had a way of making everything seem distant, small, even manageable. But the tight knot in Simon's chest wouldn't unravel that easily.

As he stood there, lost in thought, he spotted Angie walking toward him. Even from a distance, her presence made his heart lift, a warmth spreading through his veins that was welcome but still a bit unfamiliar. She smiled as she approached, and Simon smiled back. A real one this time, not the forced, hollow mask he'd grown used to wearing.

"Hey beautiful," he greeted her.

"Hey handsome," Angie replied, coming to stand beside him. She rested her elbows on the railing, mimicking his stance as her eyes searched his face. "You've done some walking today."

Simon nodded, still staring out at the horizon. "Yeah, I was feeling pretty good. I needed to clear my head."

She tilted her head slightly, studying him with gentle curiosity. "What's up, babe?"

Simon hesitated for a moment, then turned to face her fully. "I almost got a script filled today," he admitted, watching her reaction closely.

Her eyes widened with a flash of worry. "But you didn't?"

"No." He shook his head slowly. "I wanted to, but I didn't. I stood there in line, and it took everything in me not to go through with it." He sighed, running a hand through his hair. "Even though my body feels better, my brain... my brain is still stuck in this loop. Like it's on permanent short circuit."

Angie frowned, concern lining her features. "What do you mean?"

He let out a dry laugh, his eyes tired but honest. "I mean... the mouse still wants the cheese, even though he knows the cheese is tainted with poison."

Angie exhaled, understanding dawning in her expression. She reached for his hand, lacing her fingers with his. "So... you need help?"

"Yeah," Simon admitted quietly. "I need help."

Her hand tightened around his. "Like what? Meetings? Rehab?"

He shrugged, the uncertainty still gnawing at him. "Maybe. I talked to a doctor today... about methadone. It's a treatment program. They combine it with counseling. I don't know if it's the right thing, but it's worth exploring, right?"

Angie's brows furrowed, a flicker of apprehension in her eyes. "Methadone? Isn't that... isn't that just swapping one addiction for another?" Her voice was sharper than she intended, and Simon flinched slightly.

"No, it's not. It's like a helper and supervised. Just hear me out," he said, raising a hand in a calming gesture. "I don't know if it's what I need. I don't want to jump into anything without thinking it through. But... it's something, you know? Maybe it's methadone. Maybe it's meetings. I don't have all the answers right now, but I need to look at all my options. I need you to know that I'm trying to figure it out."

Angie sighed. She rubbed her temples, the stress of the past few weeks catching up to her. "I'm sorry," she murmured. "I didn't mean to jump on you like that. I'm just... I'm scared. This is all new."

"I know," Simon whispered. "We're both scared. And I get it. There's still a long way to go."

Angie nodded, blinking back the tears that threatened to spill. "Yeah. I know."

Simon looked down at their joined hands. "Recovery isn't exactly chocolates and rainbows."

A raw laugh escaped her. "No. I wish it was."

He smiled, though it didn't quite reach his eyes. "It's gonna take a long time to retrain the mouse."

"Yeah," Angie agreed. "I know, and me too."

For a moment, they stood in silence, Simon's grip tightened on her hand, his mind swirling with the realization that no matter how hard he fought, the path ahead was still uncertain.

He looked at Angie, the one constant in his chaotic life. "I don't want it to all go to shit, but even if or when..."

She cut him off gently, her voice a quiet plea. "No, babe. I don't want us to wait for the bad days. We'll fight for every good day and let's just be ok with a boring, good day."

Simon looked at her, his heart swelling with a mixture of gratitude and love that words couldn't quite express. He brought her hand to his lips, kissing it softly, a silent promise that he would keep fighting, for her and for himself.

Together, they stood side by side, watching the waves crash against the pier as the sun began to set. The future was still unknown, still fragile, but in that moment, there was a sliver of peace.

And for now, that was enough.

To Those on This Journey with Me,

Hello, my friend, and thank you. Truly. I can't fully express what it means to me that you've allowed me to share this story with you.

When I first put pencil to paper, I was just looking for an outlet, a way to make sense of all the emotions, confusion, and heartache. Writing was my way of working through it all, and I found a kind of comfort in seeing the chaos take shape on the page.

If this story hits close to home for you, my hope is that it leaves you feeling a little less alone. For every person who battles addiction, there are those standing beside them, hurting, hoping, holding on and even letting go. This story is for you, the ones left in the wake of that battle.

Your health, both physical and emotional, matters just as much as anyone else's. I know how easy it is to carry hidden scars, afraid to look too closely at what happened, afraid to speak it into the light for fear of giving it power again. Believe me, I get it. But we can't let those fears rob us of the light we fought so hard to reach. Every good day is a victory, a moment to savor.

And now, I'd like to kindly ask that you consider leaving a review. Your words will help this story reach those far and wide. It's free. It's easy. It means everything because most readers choose books based on reviews.

To leave a review, just scan the QR code or visit this link:

https://www.amazon.com/review/review-your-purchases/error?asin=B0F7J3V959

Thank you for walking this path with me. Hold on to every moment of hope, every step toward healing, and every bit of peace you find along the way. You deserve it.

With love and gratitude,

~Regina

Made in the USA
Las Vegas, NV
13 June 2025

23602487R00138